Percival Pollard

Cape of Storms

A Novel

Percival Pollard

Cape of Storms
A Novel

ISBN/EAN: 9783743367418

Manufactured in Europe, USA, Canada, Australia, Japa

Cover: Foto ©Andreas Hilbeck / pixelio.de

Manufactured and distributed by brebook publishing software (www.brebook.com)

Percival Pollard

Cape of Storms

CAPE OF STORMS
A NOVEL

BY
PERCIVAL POLLARD

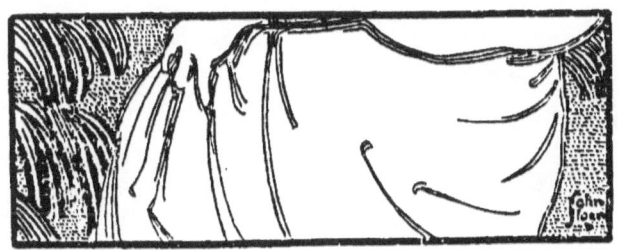

CHICAGO
THE ECHO
1895

CAPE OF STORMS

"So this old mariner, Bartholomew Diaz, called that place the cape of torments and of storms and blessed his Maker that he was safely gone by it. And even so, in the lives of us all, there is a Cape of Storms, the which to pass safely is delightful fortune, and on which to be wrecked is the common fate. For it often happens that this Corner Dangerous holds a woman's face." * * *

—An Unknown Author

1894
ST. JOSEPH
FRIDENAU
CHICAGO
1895

PROLOGUE

"LIFE is a cup that is better to sip than to drain; the taste of the dregs is very bitter in the mouth." I shall never forget those words of our dear minister's, I suppose, because so much that has happened since he first uttered them to us as we sat in his Sunday-school class has shown me the truth of them. Dick himself, I remember, was especially loth to believe Mr. Fairly's monition; indeed, none of us young bloods cared to think that there was anything in the life before us that was not altogether worth living, and when Dick spoke up plainly and quite proudly, arguing against the pastor's words, we were all silent approvers of his challenge. Dick was always the bravest boy in the village; and we had long since come to be admirers rather than rivals. But Mr. Fairly only shook his head and smiled a little—he had a wonderful smile, and his eyes were always shining with kindness—and patted Dick on the head, with a gentle, "Well, well, my boy, let us hope so; let us hope so. Perhaps you will be fortunate above your fellows."

The incident dwells in my memory for many reasons. It was, as I have said, a curiously prophetic sentence of our pastor's ; besides that, it was the last Sunday that we were all together in Lincolnville, we boys who had played, and fought and learned together. Early in the week, Dick—somehow, long after the world has come to know him only as Richard Lancaster, I am still unable to think of him as anything but the "Dick" of my boyhood—was to leave the village for the world ; he was going to begin a life for himself, up there in that mysteriously magnetic maelstrom— the town. Like Dick Whittington of old, and every fresh young blood every day of this world's life, he was going up to town to conquer. Before him lay the beautiful pathway into a glorious future ; promises and pleasures were like hedges to that way that he was going to tread. He was all eagerness, all hope, all ambition. And, to be just, perhaps there was never a boy went up to town from Lincolnville who had better cause to be full of pleasant hopes for his future than Dick. Certainly, it was the first time the little place had evolved such a talent; and it felt a pardonable pride in the boy; it expected, perhaps, even more than he did, and was looking forward to the reflected glory of being his native village.

If you have traveled through the West at all, and have anything more than a car-window acquaintance with the great Middle West, you know Lincolnville fairly well, I think. Not that you may ever have been to the village itself, but because it is a type of thousands of other villages scattered throughout the country.

It is the county-seat, and is built upon the checker-board plan, with a sort of hollow square in the middle, filled, as an Irishman might say, with a park. The sides of this square form the business heart of the place; each street that runs away from the square is lined with pretty dwelling-houses of frame or brick, so that the village looks like an octopus with four large tentacles stretching toward every point of the compass. The streets are fringed with shade trees of every sort, and in mid-summer the place looks like a veritable nest of green and cool bowers. The county is strictly and agricultural one; the farmers come to "town," as they call it, every Saturday; at least, hitch their horses to the iron railing that surrounds the park, and spend the day selling produce, buying dry goods, implements or other necessaries. The face of the village rarely changes; there is an occasional fire on the "square," mayhap, and then the newer building that fills the gap is in decided improvement over the old one; young men are forever going out into the world, and old men are for evercoming back thither to die; for the rest, one might fancy that, if you came into the world again a hundred years from now, you would find the same farmers doing their "trading" at exactly the same stores that they now favor. On occasions of a political convention, or a circus, the town takes on

3

a festive aspect, and the roads leading to the square are filled, all day long, with wagons that have come from the further edges of the county. During the three or four days of the County Fair, too, there is great activity between the village and the Fair Grounds, and, if it be a dry summer, the air between those places is merely one huge cloud of dust. Occasionally the pretty little Opera House has an entertainment that draws out such of the citizens as have no very severe religious scruples against the theatre. For the rest, the place is an admirable home of quiet. Young blood chafes at this quiet; old blood finds there the peace it seeks.

In the very nature of things, a place of this sort is chiefly concerned with its own affairs; the main theme of conversation are its own people. Everyone is perfectly acquainted with his neighbor's affairs, and not infrequently, in fact, is able to inform that neighbor of certain details relating to the latter, that had until then been unknown to him. So it was that, at the time of Dick's leaving Lincolnville, the good people of that place knew, much better than he did himself, the surety of his engagement to Dorothy Ware. He himself would have been only too glad to be as sure as they were, when he heard the rumors he was given to smiling rather sardonically.

He came to me once, I remember, and looked at me for a long time with those clear, grey eyes of his. "Tell me, old man," he said, "do you think she cares for me?" It is a stupid question, this; but almost every boy who is in love puts it to some friend or other, in the quest for confirmation of his fears or hopes. "Why, Dick," I said—still more foolishly, perhaps, now that I look back on it—"Why, Dick, of course she does. We all do." "Oh," he flung in, impatiently," "I don't mean that!" I knew what he meant; but who shall tell, being a man, whether a girl cares or not? Although, if ever a boy was made to be well beloved, surely it was Dick.

He was always a high-spirited youngster; some of his tricks are still legends of the old high-school in his native place. He never liked to fight, being naturally mild of temper; but when he was roused beyond endurance he was a veritable Daniel. His father died when he was only four years old; to his mother he was the most devoted of sons.

It was when he was about ten years old that his talent for drawing first proved itself. It came to him in the way that it has come to many who have since made the world listen to their names— on the old blackboard in the school-room. It was a caricature of Mr. Fairly, I remember, who was always very tall and very thin, and whose face was like that of a French general's under the empire. Dick exaggerated all these peculiarities most deftly with his chalk, and then it so happened that Mr. Fairly himself walked in and found the caricature. He only looked at Dick quietly, and put his hand down on his shoulder with a subdued, "I am a good deal older than you, my boy, a good deal older. You're sorry, aren't you?" And something in our minister's tone must have touched Dick, for the boy put his head down and said: "Yes, sir," with a little choke in his voice. Nor do I think that from that day to this Dick has ever drawn or painted in caricature. But in all other ways he developed his talent day by day with really wonderful results. He always had a rare notion of color; the autum foliage thereabouts gave him the most startling effects. He used to go out into the woods in mid-summer and mid-winter—it made little difference to him—and come back with some of the prettiest bits of landscape work I have ever seen. There were, it is true, certain palpable crudities in his work, due to the lack of any training save that of his instincts, but those would undoubtedly disappear as soon as he came under the influence of a proper instructor. It was for this that he was going to leave the village and become of the greater world in town. His mother had rebelled at first; she was growing old, and she feared the thought of losing sight of him; but there was no restraining his ambition. To remain cooped up in that little corral of a place all his life—oh, no; that was not at all the thing for Dick Lancaster. That great world, out there, that he had read and heard so much about, that was where he ought to be; and it was there he wanted to wager and to win; what was there left in Lincolnville? He could do nothing more there; his life was beginning to be a mere stagnation. He must out and away. This longing for shaking off the shackles of that narrow village life was, as much as ambition, the spur that sent him out into the larger world. And I do not wonder at him. Those small places are not fit arenas for the disporting of ambitions or freedoms.

At this time, Dick was a little over one-and-twenty. He was handsome in a dark, olive-skinned sort of way, and his eyes had the longest lashes I have ever seen in a man. His hair curled a little, though he was forever trying to comb and coax the curl away; he hated it, saying that curls were all right for a girl, perhaps, but not for a man. He was, but for the fact that he was very fond of good cigars, a veritable Pierrot. He had always been very closely under his mother's influence; even his association with the boys of his own age and class had not been enough to taint him at all. He had a fancy that, now as I consider it, after all these years, seems a most pathetic one, that the world was a very beautiful place in which the wicked were always punished, if not by actual stripes, at least by the disdain of their fellowmen. It seems strange, perhaps, that a young man of his age should still hold such notions, but you must remember that in the quieter villages of our country it is possible to hold these fancies all one's life; the town is the great disenchanter. Dick considered that he had two things to live for —his ambition and Dorothy Ware.

It was beautiful, the way the boy sometimes rhapsodized; beautiful, and yet in the light of after events, sad. "One day, you know," he said in one of his bursts of enthusiasm, "I will be known all the world over as a great painter. People will come to my studio and wonder at it, and the work in it. They will invite me everywhere. I will be a lion. But I shall always place my work first; admiration shall go into the last place. And there will be Dorothy! Dear Dorothy! I haven't asked her yet, you know, but I hope—oh, yes, I hope—that it will be all right between us. Dorothy will help me in everything; when I begin to flag, or to lose spirit, she will spur me on. She will represent me to the great world of society when I am hard at work; she will be my veritable Alter Ego. And some day—some day, when I feel that my brush and my hand have in them the passion for my masterpiece, I will paint her face—her face !" He took up a photograph that lay on the table before him and looked at it steadily for an instant or two. "Sweet face !" he went on, "how shall mere paint ever represent you ? There must be love, too. Love and paint. The one is a mere trick of the hand and eye; the other is mine and mine alone. For no one can love her as I do."

As for Miss Dorothy Ware, she was eighteen and beautiful. I do not know that any woman really needs a fuller description than that. As for her wit, it is too early in this chronicle to speak of that; nor do I, personally, differ much from Theophile Gautier, when he states that a woman who has wit enough to be beautiful has all she needs.

Miss Ware's father had made a great deal of money by the very simple process of growing old; he had been one of the pioneer settlers in that county and his had been most of the land that the village now stood on. Miss Ware herself, while sensible of her riches, was unspoilt by them. By nature she was of the disposition that one can call nothing else but "sweet;" she was tender and gracious; she was fond of fun, so long as that fun annoyed no one else; in a word, she was considerate and gentle and lovable. She had been brought up in the south, and she had retained a trace of the southern accent, so that her speech was in itself a charm; she had natural talents for looking pretty under all circumstances; some might have said that she had the instincts of a coquette, but I do not believe it of her. She was devoted to children and dumb animals. And whoso has those instincts is intrinsically good. But Miss Ware held that she had by no means had enough of this world's pleasures to begin thinking of so solemn a thing as marriage. Like a large number of the girls of today, she was, first and foremost, "out for a good time," as the slang of the time has it. She had certainly the intention of some day marrying the man she loved and making him as happy as she could; but in the meanwhile she wanted to test the world's ability to furnish entertainment quite a little while yet. Which was why, although she was very fond of Dick, she had invariably put him off, when he grew importunate, with a laugh. "Why, Dick," she would say, "don't you know you're absurd to think of such a thing? We're just children yet. Oh, I know we're of age, but what of that? You don't mean to tell me that you think your life has shaped, or even begun to shape itself yet? No. And as for me, I'm going to skirmish around a while yet before I settle down and become old married people! Be sensible, Dick!" And Dick, with a sigh in his heart, was, perforce, fain to say that he would try. "Skirmish around!" It grated on him, somehow, that phrase; it seemed to hold for him visions of innumerable flirtations; of contact with the world, the flesh and the devil, with the brushing off of the faint, roseate bloom of innocence.

It was on the day before Dick's departure for town that Lincolnville received the news of another intended going abroad. The Wares' were to sail for Europe before the month was out. Mrs. Ware had long been an invalid; for years the doctors had advised travel, but her husband's objections to any sort of change had hitherto prevailed against her wishes. But now the really dangerous state of Mrs. Ware's health, added to the entreaties of Dorothy, who longed, as do all American girls, for a glimpse of the old country, had brought the old gentleman to acquiescence. He would not go himself; he was getting too old for such a trip; but his wife and daughter should go, if they had set their hearts on it. So that, with the prospective departure of both Richard Lancaster and the girl that rumor had him engaged to, the tongues of the gossips had plenty to do on that day. When Dick first heard the news about the Wares' he was inclined to be downhearted; then it struck him that it would give him an opportuity for another effort at getting from Dorothy at least the promise of a promise.

Than Lincolnville in mid-summer I know few fairer places; there is a cool, green quiet all about that makes for peace and gentleness, and in the whispering of the breeze as it curls through the thick foliage of the spreading trees there is the note of happiness. Happiness, indeed, lies nearer to man in one of these small, serene villages, than anywhere else in the world, save in solitude; but it is rarely that man sees the sleeping beauty that he has sought all his life long. Dick, as he walked along toward the Ware house that splendid afternoon, caught something of the warm, comfortable languor that was in the air, and looked about him with a note of regret in his regard. "How pretty it all is!" he thought, looking at the familiar houses, with their well-kept lawns and ivy-covered verandahs, "how pretty! And yet—" he sighed, and then smiled with a proud lift of the head— "there are other things!"

He found Miss Ware seated in a hammock on what was known as the front-porch. It was a long, low, cool stretch of verandah, reminding one of the style of architecture in vogue in the old south. It was all harbored in vines that were so luxurious they hardly gave the breeze a fair chance to penetrate; on the other hand, the sun's rays were safely guarded against.

Young Lancaster drew up a chair, after she had smiled and reached him one of her hands. He looked at her critically for a moment.

"Dorothy," he said, "I have never seen you looking so pretty."

"I have never felt so happy, Dick," she said.

"Because you are going away?"

"Yes. And you?"

"I am happy, too. And yet, I am rather sorry. I have lived here all my life; this is the first time that I am going away from home. There is something solemn about it; but then—the end, oh, the end—justifies it all. That is not the chief reason why I am not altogether satisfied to go away. Dorothy, don't you know the other reason?"

She opened her eyes a little, and smiled a trifle at the corners of her mouth. "I, Dick, why, how should I know?" Then she saw that he looked hurt and she changed her tone. "Dick," she went on, "why won't you be sensible about it? I suppose you mean about me? Why, Dick, you know I like you, don't you? I've always liked you and admired you, but—dear me, can I help it if I feel sure that I don't like anyone yet—in that way? I'd like to, perhaps, but—well, I don't. What can I do?" She looked at him appealingly and reproachfully.

"I know, I know," he said, soothingly, "I'm an impetuous, thoughtless idiot, I'm afraid, and I hurt you. And, oh, Dorothy! don't you know I'd rather suffer torments unspeakable than hurt you?" He put out his hand and touched the one hand of hers that swung beside him, over the edge of the hammock. "But yet, dear," he went on, "if I only had a word from you to remember, be it ever so slight, I would fight so much better against the world. For it is the same to-day as it was in the middle ages; we go to our crusades, all of us, and if we have a sweetheart who will give us her love as an armor, we fight the better fight. Our crusades have a different air, to be sure, but the idea is the same. Don't you know, Dorothy, that if you only gave me some little thing to cling to, I would feel a hundred times stronger. Come, Dorothy, it costs you little to say it!"

"But if I say that word, I must live up to it."

"True; your fair conscience would let you do nothing less. And yet, there are words so slight that they would cost you scarcely anything, while to me they would be coats of mail."

For a time there was silence, both looking out over the street where the school children were passing homewards. A buggy rattled by, throwing clouds of dust; then there was quiet again. "If you could say to me, Dorothy, 'Dick, I won't marry anyone until I see you again, until I come home again. And I'll try to like you—that way,' why, that would be enough for me."

She held up her right hand with a pretty little gesture. "I do solemnly swear," she said. Then she went on more seriously, "Why, yes, Dick, I'll promise that. Small chance of my getting married for a few years, anyway, so I won't have such a very awful time living up to that promise. Now, do you think, sir, that you're engaged to me?"

"No, no, dear; not at all. But you've let me hope, haven't you? That's all I want. You don't know how much happier I'll feel all the time you're away. How long, by the way, do you think you'll be abroad?"

"A year, at the least. I want to see it all, you know, when I do get the chance. Mamma'll want to stay in Carlsbad or Ems, or somewhere all the time; but I'm going to get her well real soon, you see if I don't, and then we'll just travel for fun and nothing else. Dick, wouldn't it be great if you could go along?"

"It would, for a fact," he assented, "but it's too good to be true. Besides I'm going to have some fun of my own!"

"Your work, you mean?"

"Yes. Isn't it fun to succeed? And I'm going to succeed! The fighting for success will be fun, and the victory will be fun!" His eyes flashed with a fierce battle-light. Today this fire of ambition is the only thing that at all takes the place of the blood fervor that spurred on the knights of the olden times.

"Dorothy," he said, presently, with a sudden softness in his voice," "will you wish me luck?"

She gave him, for answer, her right hand, and looked at him wistfully. She was wondering, perhaps, why it was that she did not love this lovable boy. "I wish you all the success in the world," she said quietly. And then, as he turned to go, she called after him, in the old formula they had used to each other a thousand times as boy and girl— "Good-bye, Dick. Be good!"

The love affairs of a boy and a girl, you may think, are hardly the things that matter very much in the world of today. But the boy and girl of today are the man and the woman of tomorrow; and between these stages there is only the little gulf, so easily crossed, wherein runs the river of knowledge of the world we live in. As soon as we have crossed that we are become men and women, and are left of our childhood nothing but the wish that it were ours again.

CHAPTER I

ALTHOUGH the western windows were open, it was decidedly warm in the offices of the *Weekly Torch*. The offices were on the tenth floor in one of the town's best known sky-scrapers — the Aurora. There was a view, through the windows, of innumerable roofs and streets; here and there the tower of a railway station or a new hotel protruded—in the words of A. B. Wooton owner of the *Torch*—"like a sore thumb." Mr. Wooton was at that moment engaged in the diverting pastime of having his feet stretched over the side of his desk; and watching the smoke of his cigarette curl out of the window. Besides his own, there were three other desks, of the roller-top pattern, in the room, the door of which was marked "Editorial Rooms," but was rarely, if ever, seen closed. As a usual thing the outer door to the corridor was, in the summer-time at least, also left wide open; you could see from the window clear to the outer door. Indeed, it was one of Wooten's special talents, this ability of his to see at a glance, from his seat by the window, who it was that was coming in through the farther door. At one of the other desks a man was smoking a pipe and shoving a pencil rapidly over sheet of paper. Presently this man laid his pencil down, took his pipe out of his mouth and knocked the ashes over into the cuspidor. Then he leaned back in his chair and inquired,

"Who was it?"

"Young fellow from the Art Institute," said Wooten. "Sketches to show; wants to do illustrating; same old gag. They all come to it. Paint and fame come altogether too high, and a fellow's got to live. Although, as the Frenchman remarked, '*Je ne vois pahs la necessite.*'" The ability to hideously mispronounce French with a sort of bravado that almost made it seem correct was one of Wooten's peculiarities.

16

The other man gave a mock shudder. "If your morals," he said, "were as bad as your French, you would't be fit to print. Was his stuff any good?"

"Very fair. Got a thing or two to learn about working for reproduction, as all these art-school men have; but he's got it in him. I told him to go and see young Belden, on the *Chronicle*, to get a few points about reproduction. I believe I'll be able to use him. If he's cheap." Wooton laughed, and threw the stub of his cigarette out of the window. Then he began throwing the papers on his desk all in a heap and looking into, under and around them. "Confound the luck," he began; then, turning to the other man, "Got a cigarette, Van?"

Van, whose full name was Vanstruther, and whom his intimates called alternately "Tom" and "Van," threw a box over to the other's desk, laughing. "I swear," he said, "it's my firm belief that if a man were to put you in a story and try to draw you with a single stroke he would only have to say that you spent your life between buying and losing cigarettes."

"And matches," added the other calmly. "Got one?"

"Jupiter! If this thing goes on I'm going to strike for higher rates. It's not in the contract that I furnish the office with smokes!"

"No. But the stuff you write, Van, is what drives me to cigarettes. So you make your own bed, you see. Hallo!

Here's a lone female to see me! Wonder who?

He got up and went towards the door. "Did you wish to see me?" he inquired.

"The editor?" She hesitated a little but he assured her with a slight nod that she had found her man, and she followed him towards his desk. She took a seat beside him, and they began conversing in a tone so low that Vanstruther could only catch a stray word now and again. Presently she got up. "Very well then," she was saying, "you have my address; if anything should turn up, you will let me know, won't you?" With a little rustling of skirts she was gone. Presently they could here her voice saying "Down!" to the elevator boy.

"What was her game?" asked Vanstruther.

"Wanted to contribute poetry as a regular department. You can't fling a club around a corner anywhere in this town without hitting one of her kind, nowadays!"

"Then why didn't you tell her right away you weren't using anything of that sort?"

"Why, you infernal idiot, didn't you look at her?"

"No. Choice?"

"Very." He put a slip of paper into a pigeon hole, remarking as he did so, "Filed for future reference."

From the next room came a gruff voice, "Column of editorial to fill yet, Mr. Wooton."

"That foreman of mine's like Banquo's ghost," muttered Wooton, as he put his pen into the ink and bent down over the desk. For a while there was only the sound of pen and pencil going over paper, and the click of the type in the next room. Then there was a heavy step heard in the passage outside, and presently Wooton muttered: . "The Lord's giving us this day our daily loafers, I see. I wonder why it is," he went on aloud, as a tall, heavy-set man, with a military mustache and eyeglasses in front of mild blue eyes, came into the room, "that you fellows always show up on Friday. Which, being the day we go to press—what's that? More copy? Oh, all right!" The foreman was taking all the written sheets from his desk· and pleading for more. The new comer was evidently used to this sort of greeting; he calmly picked a cigarette from the box on Vanstruther's desk, lit it and sat down on a chair that was drawn up to the table·where the "exchanges" lay piled in heaps. He final'y found what he had been apparently looking for—a paper with a very gaudy and risky picture on the front of the cover; he folded it to his satisfaction and began to look through it. "Say, Van," he began, presently, "what's this I hear about their going to play the Ober-Ammergau Passion Play here? Anything in it?"

Vanstruther was terribly busy. "Haven't heard," was all he said.

"I heard that it was all fixed," the other went on. "They've even got the man to play the leading part. Fellow called Tom Vanstruther. They say he's going to play the part without a make-up, and—"

"Oh, look here," said Vanstruther, half turning around in his chair, "you go to the devil, will you?"

The other man took out a huge cigar-holder, inserted his cigarette and curled his mustache. "Van's still a little sore about that," he said, turning to Wooton, who merely nodded his head. There came again the sound of footsteps in the outer hall, and Wooton, peering forward a little, broke into a cheery "Hallo, Dante Gabriel Belden, glad to see you! Come in. By the way, I just sent a young fellow who has your disease over to see you this morning. Wants to learn the reproduction rules of the game. See him?"

"Yes. Had a little talk with him. Clever chap. Tell you about him in a minute. Hallo, Van, how are the other three hundred and ninety-nine? Hallo, Stanley, haven't they got you under the vagrancy ordinance yet?"

The man with the huge mustache and the lengthy cigar-holder shook his head and said, "Not yet. But I understand they're on the trail. Well, how is Art, and what are the books you have lately bought, and what is the latest of your schemes that has died?"

"Oh, give them to me one at a time. Hang it, Wooton, why do you allow this man to come up here, anyway, to wear out your furniture and the patience of us all?"

"Oh," said Wooton, "he's an amusing

animal, and I forgive any man anything
if only he will amuse me."

"That's beastly bad morals!" said
the artist.

"Morals!" echoed Wooton, with a
bland smile, "my dear boy, you want to
take a pill. No; take two! Morals in
this day and age; moreover, on the
borders of Bohemia, to talk about morals! Jove, I see myself forced to seek
the solace of the deadly cigarette."
He lit one of those slender rolls of
tobacco and paper and went on, "However you haven't answered Stanley's
questions yet. For you must know,
Van, that Belden is one of the most extravagant and insatiable hunters of art
books in all this town. Ever been in
his flat? Well, it's a series of rooms,
completely lined with books and pictures, with a very small hole in the
middle of each room. Said hole being
usually filled—to use an Irishism—with
a center-table loaded to the guards with
art portfolios. I don't believe there's a
book or art store in town that the man
doen't owe large bills to; and I know,
for a fact, that when it comes to be a
question between a new overcoat and a
new art book, he always takes the latter. And as for his schemes—well, I
will admit they're all good, but, like the
good, they die young. While they have
the merit of exceeding novelty, they
ride him like the plague; but presently
a new idol comes and the old one falls
into decay. Tell us, Dante, about the
newest scheme!"

"H'm," replied the artist, "I don't

see that you've left me anything to tell.
I've got a new book of Vierge's stuff that
you fellows want to come up and see
one of these days; that's about all that
I can think of."

"Thank you for the pressing invitation," said Wooton.

"Oh, and about that fellow you sent
up to see me," Belden continued, "I
liked his stuff immensely. He needs a
little experience and hard luck on the
practical side of getting his stuff made
into cuts, and he'll be all right. The
fact is, Wooton, seeing you like the fellow's sketches fairly well, and I'm rushed
to death with other work, I've thought
of turning my work for the *Torch* over to
him. Would you object?"

"Not a bit, provided he does it as
well; and he won't have to get much of
a move on to do that. And then they're
cheaper when they're green!"

Belden groaned. "You're the most
awful specimen of materialism I ever
hope to run up against. Then you
don't object to this fellow––what's his
name again, Lancaster, isn't it?––doing
your sketches? All right, I'll train him
a bit for you. And then I guess it
would be a good scheme for him to have
a desk here in your office somewhere, so
that he can have a workshop and be
right at hand for you. It isn't as if he
had a studio of his own."

"That'll be all right; we've got plenty
of room. But while you're training
him, old man, I hope you won't inocu-
late him with that villainous style of
dressing you adopt at the end of your

pen. You're very hot people on everything that's got to be done in a hurry, and you're great on fine work of the etching order, but when it comes to making people look like the men and women one would care to be seen with, you're simply not in this county, that's all there is about it. I've always claimed, you know," he went on, turning a little so that he faced Vanstruther and Stanley, "that the great fault common to all the black-and-white artists in this town was that they couldn't define the difference between a gentleman and a hoodlum. They talk to me about technique, and drawing, and all the rest of it, none of which, I will admit, I know a mortal thing about; but all I answer is that I'm going from the point of view of the man who doesn't know how the drawing is made, but who does know how it looks when it's finished. The people of today look at nearly everything for it's merely superficial aspect; and the finer people look to our artists to display taste in clothing their pictorial creatures. If you only dress your people well, they'll want your drawings so that they can get fashion pointers from them. Now-a-days an illustrator has got to be more than a mere manipulator of pen and ink; he has got to keep an eye on the fashions, and even a little ahead of them. At least, that's what the man I'm looking for should be."

Stanley muttered, around the edges of his mustache, so that only Vanstruther could hear, "Yes; and he'd want to pay him as much as ten dollars a week!"

Belden laughed, and got up. "Why don't you put all that into a lecture, Wooton, and give the fellows over at the Institute a glimpse of this higher knowledge of yours. However, I've got to be going. I'll send that man Lancaster over here in a day or so. Goodbye, people!"

"There's one of the cleverest fellows with a pen in this town," said Wooten, as soon as the artist's footsteps had died away down the corridor, "but he's utterly spoiled himself by the work he's been doing of late years. He's a very fast worker, and one of the best men a daily paper ever got hold of. Then, too, I've seen copy-work of his—that is, from photographs or paintings—done in pen-and-ink, that had all the fine detail and effect of an etching. But, for the sake of the money there is in it, he does blood and thunder illustrations for a paper of that sort. After a man has done that sort of thing for a year or two, it gets into his style. I don't believe he'll ever be able to do anything else, now. Of course, he'll aways make good money, because his speed and capacity for work are simply invaluable; but art, as far as he is concerned, must be weeping large salty tears."

"This picture of you, A. B. Wooton, pleading the cause of art," remarked Stanley, "is one of the most affecting I have ever beheld. It really makes me feel—hungry."

"Your invitation, sir," said Wooton, walking over toward the closet and getting his hat, "is cordially accepted. Come on, Van; we are invited to lunch by the Honorable Mr. Stanley, exchange reader to the *Torch*. Never linger in a case like this!"

"For consummate nerve," Stanley suggested, "you really take the medal, A. B. However, seeing I made a little borrow from the old lady yesterday, I will go you one lunch on the strength of it. But I do hope you men had late breakfasts."

Just before they were ready to pass out, Tony, the office boy came in. "Say," he said to Wooton, in a low tone, "you remember that letter I took to the house day before yesterday? Well, does the quarter walk to-day?"

"Which," Wooton explained, as he handed the boy a quarter, "is Tony's peculiar way of inquiring whether he is going to get that twenty-five cents or not." Tony grinned and went back to his desk were he was busy addressing wrappers.

When the three men came back from lunch, they found a young man, holding a black leather case in his hand, such as bank messengers carry, sitting patiently in a chair in the outer office. He got up when they entered, and handed Wooton a paper. Wooton took it to the light, read it slowly, and handed it back. "Tell him to send that around again on the tenth, will you." Then he walked into the composing room and began talking to the foreman. The collector put the slip of paper back into his portfolio and went out.

"Van," said Wooton, as they sat down at his desk, presently, "I wish you'd try and hurry that stuff of yours along a little, will you? I've got to go to a tea at Mrs. Stewart's at four, and the ghost tells me that your page is half a column shy yet."

Vanstruther nodded silently, while Stanley inquired, "Excuse my ignorance Mr. Wooten, but who is Mrs. Stewart?"

"What? You don't know the great and only Annie McCallum Stewart? Oh, misericordia, can such things be?"

"They are."

"Well, Mrs. Stewart is a remarkably clever woman. One of the cleverest women our society affords, in fact. She is the daughter of one of the town's best known and most popular doctors, and everyone in society knew her so well when she was only Annie McCallum that now, when she is married to Stewart, one still uses her old name as well as her new one. That's all the result of individuality. She has read a great deal, and kept her eyes open a great deal. She has a husband who is ridiculously fond of her, and otherwise as blind as a bat. She, on the other hand, has a mania for young men. Whenever you see her with a young man of any sort of looks, somebody will tell you that Annie McCallum Stewart has got a new youth in the net. She likes to lure them up into her 'den,' as she calls it, and talk to them about the higher life. Then they fall in love with her and she forgives them and elaborates upon the beauties of pure Platonism. In a word, Stanley, she's

26

one of the most perfect forms of the mental flirt I ever come across."

"H'm. Is your tea today to be in duet form, or is it a general scramble?"

"Oh, it's a general all-comers' game. But I always like to go to that house; she interests me immensely. I'm always wondering how near she really can skate to the edge without breaking over."

"Yes," acquiesced the other, reflectively, "that is an interesting speculation. Hallo, here's another friend of yours!"

The new-comer laid an envelope on Wooton's desk and waited. The latter opened it hastily, and then said, "I sent that down by this morning's mail."

The man had hardly gone before Stanley laid down the paper he had been paging through and said, looking steadily at Wooton, "Jupiter, but you do that easily! If I could do that only half as well I'd count myself as free from debts for the rest of my life. It's my solemn belief that you can tell a collector from an ordinary mortal as soon as he steps inside the door. I've heard you tell a man, who had only just turned inside the outer office, that you were 'going to send that down in the morning,' and I've seen you look the enemy calmly in the face and tell him that you had fixed that up with his employer about an hour ago. And you do it as easily as if you were lighting a cigarette. Another man might get embarrassed, and hesitate, or feel guilty! But you! Not in a hundred years! You never quail worth a cent. It's positive genius, my boy, positive genius!"

"No; it's only business, that's all."

"H'm, by the way, speaking of business, aren't you running the game a trifle extravagantly here? I don't want to mix in, of course, but is the thing paying so well as—"

The other interrupted him. "My dear fellow," he said, "it's evident you haven't any idea how well this thing is paying. Why, man, look at me! Do I economise much? No. Well, I don't have to, that's why! But come on and let's saunter down street. Van's finished, and they've got all the copy they want, and I expect there are a few pretty girls out today. Let's go and take a glimpse at the parade on the Avenue. And then I'll go down to that tea."

There were several callers at the office after they had left; some bill-collectors, a society man who left the announcement for some forthcoming dances; a boy to buy ten copies of last week's paper; a printer looking for work; and the mail-carrier. Towards six o'clock the foreman and the compositors left; then Tony, the office-boy, shut up his desk, and went out, locking the door behind him. The *Weekly Torch* had gone to rest for the day.

CHAPTER II

IN the very air and life that prevailed in the office of the *Torch* there was, as one may suppose, something strange, and at first repugnant to Dick Lancaster. To one of his bringing

up, his earnest intentions, his thirst for
real things, it seemed that all this was very
like a gaudy sham, a bubble of pretense,
of surface prattle. He could scarcely
believe that the flippancy of these men
was serious with them; their talk, their
point of view astonished and horrified
him. If they were to be believed, life
was nothing but a skimming of more or
less uneven surfaces; the only thing to
be tried for was pleasure, and there was
no moral line at all. And then again he
rebuked himself for being, perhaps, a
homesick young idiot, overgiven to morbid speculation. That was not what he
had come to town for; he was going to
do some good work and make a name
and fame for himself.

He had found, very early in his career,
that in order to get upon the first steps
of the ladder he must become an illustrator. If he had had the means that
would have enabled him to wait through
studio-work, a trip to Paris, and the
dreary years ere orders came from deal-
ers, he would have clung to paint at any
risk; but he saw himself forced to earn
some bread-and-butter even while he
waited for his dreams to come true. So,
with some slight reluctance at first, to be
sure, but afterwards with all his energy,
he applied himself to pen and ink work.
In course of time, as we have seen, he
became the staff-artist of the *Torch*.
He was making a very fair living for so
young a man, and he made a great many
acquaintances. And life every day
showed him a new aspect.

One of the men he had so far taken

the greatest liking to was Belden, the
artist, who had, to all intents and pur-
poses, put him into his present position
with the *Torch*. Belden, whose name
was Daniel Grant Belden, but whom
his friends chaffingly called, on account
of the similarity of the initials, Dante
Gabriel, was one of the most happy-
go-lucky individuals that ever breathed.
His mania for art books kept him
more or less hard-up; yet he undoubtedly had one of the finest
collections, in that sort, in town.
He got orders for work from a publisher;
he took the manuscript that he was to
illustrate home with him; he kept it
three weeks; then, without having read
it, he returned it saying he was too busy
to attempt the commission. And if
ever there was one in this present day
of ours, he was a Bohemian. The
peculiar part of it was that in addition
to being a Bohemian by instinct, he was
one by intention. He read Henri
Murger with avidity, and thought of
him always. On the street he was a
curious object; his overcoat was a trifle
shiny, and his hat was always an old,
or at least, a misused one; his trousers
were too tight at the knees; his boots
rarely polished. He usually walked
with a long, quick stride; and a long,
peculiar cigar, of the sort the Wheeling
people call "stogy," was almost always
in his mouth. You rarely saw him on
the Elevated except with an armful of
books and papers. He would come
home at one in the morning and sit
down at his wide drawing table and work

until dawn. Then, with not much more than his coat hastily thrown off, he would fling himself on the couch and be fast asleep in an instant. Often, too, he would go fast to sleep while his pen was traveling over the paper; in ten minutes, or sometimes half an hour, he would wake up and continue the stroke that had been interrupted; his pen would have not spilled a single drop. He did all his own cooking, and marvelous were the meals that resulted. He liked nothing better than to fill his rooms with a number of choice, congenial souls. They would talk art-shop for hours, or listen to music; he knew a great many clever young fellows who were gifted in playing the piano, the flute or the violin; and while his own musical tastes were barbaric, and called, chiefly, for the spirited rendition of darky-minstrelsies, he gave the rest of his company the freedom of their choice, also, and sat patiently through the most beautiful of operatic strains. Sunday was the day singled out more especially for those pleasant little "evenings" at Belden's flat.

Dick Lancaster had been asked up to these evenings a great many times before he ever went. For long, he could not make up his mind to it; in spite of all the thousand and one laxities that he saw in the daily life around him, to devote oneself to anything in the nature of sheer pleasure, on Sunday, still seemed to him a decided mis-step.

But one day, toward the beginning of winter, Belden, who had been in to call on his young protegee at the *Torch* office, said to him,

"Look here, Dick, why don't you come up some Sunday evening and join our gang? Goodness, you can't afford to be as straight-laced as all that, in this town. Besides, we don't do anything that's against the law and the prophets, you know. We talk a little shop, and some man reads something, perhaps, and Stanley plays a thing or two on the violin. Then we go out and help ourselves to whatever I may happen to have in the larder. And then you go home, or you bunk up there, and where's the harm done? Look at it sensibly, my boy; we are all slaves in the same bondage, in this town, and Sunday is our one off-day; you don't mean to say we're heathens and creatures of the devil if we seek the sweetest rest we can on that day? To some men, rest means church; to me and most of the men you know, it means relaxation, and relaxation means recreation. The others get their music in church, I get mine at home. Now, Dick, say you'll come up next Sunday."

And Dick, looking at Belden as if to make out whether that artist were an emissary of the Evil One or merely a man of the present day, coughed a little, and then said, rather sheepishly, "Very well, I'll come—to please you, Belden." He felt, the next minute, as if he had slipped and fallen; he grew a little faint; he thought he could hear the sound of the church bells as they used to come singing over the meadows in Lincolnville; he saw himself and his mother sitting side by side in the old pew, listening to the pleasant voice of Mr. Fairly droning out his prayer; then he shook himself together and blushed at his fancies. Belden had gone already, but Dick felt as if he would run after him and tell him, "No, no, I cannot, must not come!" He ran to the door; the corridor was empty; Belden was half way down the next block by this time. Then he solaced himself with the thought, "Surely it can be no great harm after all — besides, I have promised!"

He bent down over the drawing-board once more, but he could no longer chain his thoughts to the work before him. They flew round and round in a curious circling way about this new life that he had become a part of. It was, he was forced to admit to himself, not as beautiful a thing as he had expected; but it was certainly novel, and it interested him immensely, it kept his curiosity excited, it touched his senses. As he began to consider that quiet country village that he had left, out yonder on the plains, and this busy beehive of a metropolis, he came, also, to consider the men he was beginning to know. He leaned back in the chair, smiling a little. The office was nearly empty at this time; it was during the noon hour, and Dick was alone in the outer office. He passed over, in his thoughts, the men that he was thrown with in the *Torch* office. There was Wooton himself: tall, thin, with a face that was

all profile—a wonderfully pure profile—
with a mouth almost too small for a
man, a nose that bent a little like those
of the Cæsars. Dick did not know,
yet, what to make of Wooton. The
man had a wonderful charm; he could
talk most entertainingly, most logically
and he had some curiously interesting
theories. There was a sort of *laisser-
aller* negligence in his manner; his
manners were admirable, and there was
some occult fascination about him that
one could scarcely· define. As Dick
considered him, he remembered that on
several occasions, he had listened to
Wooton's dissertations on subjects that
otherwise would have offended him,
merely because the man's charm of person and speech were so alluring. As to
whether it was genuine or a mere
veneer, well, how could one tell as soon
as this? Time, which tells so many
things, would doubtless tell that too.

Then Vanstruther! He had a blonde
beard that came to a point, and he
always wore glasses. For the rest,
Dick knew but little of him save what
he had heard. Vanstruther "did" the
more important of the society events
for the *Torch*, and himself moved and
had his nightly being in the smartest
circles in town. The peculiar part of it
was that he was married, and had
several children; barring the hour or so
a day that he spent in the office of the
Torch he was the most devoted
husband and father in the world, and
spent the most of his day at home,
where in his little study-room he sat in

front of a typewriter stand and manufactured at lightning speed—what do
you suppose?—dime novels. This was,
among the man's intimates, a more or
less open secret; but to the world at
large, and particularly the world of
society, he was known merely as a
delightful person, socially, and something of a flaneur, intellectually.

As for Stanley—the man's full name
was Laurence Stanley—Dick had somehow taken a dislike to him. He knew
little of him except that he was a professional do-nothing, who lived off his
wife's money, speculated occasionally,
and appeared a great deal in society. No
one ever saw his wife, who was an invalid. He talked with inveterate cynicism; it was this that made him repugnant to young Lancaster. He had a
sneer and a cigarette always with him,
and Dick hated both.

The tip-tapping of a light foot-step
over the oil-cloth brought Dick back
from the land of day-dreams. It was
rather a pretty woman that stood before
him, and she was gowned in a manner
that even with his inexperience he knew
to be distinctly up-to-date, and that he
certainly admitted as attractive from an
artistic standpoint. She looked past
him into the inner office, lifted her eyebrows a trifle and inquired: "Is Mr.
Wooton not in?"

"Not just now," responded Dick, getting up, "but he will be back in a very
little while. If you would care to
wait—" He took hold of the back of a
revolving chair that stood close by.

35

"No," she declared, "I only had a
minute. Will you tell him Mrs. Stewart
was up? Or, stay; I'll write him a line."

Dick gave her some letterheads, and
pen and ink; she sat down at his desk
and began writing, with a good deal of
scratching and scraping. "There," she
said when she had addressed the envelope, "If you will please give him that
as soon as he comes in. Thank you.
Do you do this?" She pointed with one
gloved finger to the drawing he had been
busy on. He bowed silently. She
looked at him with a quick, comprehen-
sive glance, smiled a trifle, and swept
out of the door.

"So that is Mrs. Annie McCallum
Stewart!" was Dick's first mental exclamation, "well, she's certainly not an ordinary woman. Wonder if I'll ever get
to know her?"

With which speculation he turned to
his work. When Wooton returned, and
had read the note, he broke into a low
chuckle, "That's like her! Just like her.
What do you suppose she says?"

Dick was the only other person in the
outer office, so he was forced to take the
question as addressed to himself. "I
have no idea," he declared.

"She says she is getting awfully tired
of her present lot of young men, and
wants me, for goodness sake, to bring
down some one different, and bring him
soon. She says she is tired to death of
the man who has lived and seen and
heard everything, and she is dying for a
man who is as like Pierrot as two peas!"
Wooton tore the letter up mechanically,

and put the pieces into the waste-basket.
"Well," he went on, "I wish I could—"
he stopped and looked at Dick, breaking
out the next instant into a broad grin,
"Jupiter!" he added, "you're just the
man! Do you want to join the noble
army of martyrs in ordinary to the extraordinary Annie? She'll do you lots of
good; she'll be a pocket education in the
philosophy of today, and she'll put you
through all manner of interesting paces.
Seriously, she's a woman who can do a
man a lot of good, socially. And society never does a man much harm; it
broadens him, and gives him finish.
Now, you're just the sort of youth she'll
like immensely; and yet she'll soon find
out that you've heard about her and her
ways. Never mind; she won't like you
any the worse for that; she's too much a
woman of the world. What do you
think? The next time I go down to tea
at her house I'll take you along, eh?
All you've got to do is to be clever and
amusing and different to the others;
Mrs. Stewart is like the rest of society
in that she demands something of the
people she takes up, but she doesn't demand such impossibilities. I'll write
and tell her I've got the very man!" He
went on into the inner office, before Dick
had time to say anything in reply. And,
to tell the truth, the idea rather interested him. He had seen her, and had
felt interested in her; he had heard so
much about her; and now he was going
to meet her! As to being clever and
amusing, he thought he was likely to
fail miserably; but he might, uncon-

sciously perhaps, succeed in being what
Wooten called "different."

Just then Wooton gave a sudden exclamation. "This is Wednesday, isn't
it? Well, that is her afternoon. You'd
better shut up your desk for today; go
up to your rooms and get an artistic
twirl or two to your locks, and then come
down to the smoking-room of the Cosmopolitan Club about quarter to four;
I'll be there waiting for you. Then we'll
go on down to Mrs. Stewart's together."

CHAPTER III

THE days were getting very short
now, and darkness was already
hovering over the town as Dick
passed through the portals of the
Cosmopolitan. When they came out
together, Wooton and he, it seemed
to Dick that the town was in one
of its most characteristic tempers.
It was in the beginning of winter; the
air was a little damp, and smoke hung
in it so that it begrimed in an incredibly
short space of time. The buildings,
in the twilight that was half of the day's
natural dusk and half the murkiness of
the smoke, loomed against the hardly
defined sky like some towering, threatening genii. The electric lights were
beginning to peer through the gloom.
The sidewalks were alive with a never-
tiring throng, men and women jostling
each other, never stopping to apologize;
all intent not so much on the present
as on something that was always just a

38

little ahead. This, the onlooker mused, was what it meant to "get ahead," a blind physical rush in the dark, a callous indifference to others, a selfish brutality, a putting into effect the doctrine of the survival of the fittest. The streets clanged with the roll of wheels; carriages with monograms on the panels rolled by with clatter of chains and much spattering of mud; huge drays drawn by four, and sometimes six-horse teams, and blazening to the world the name of some mercantile genius whom soap or pork had enriched, thundered heavily over the granite blocks; the roar and underground buzz of the cable mingled with the deafening ringing of the bell that announced the approach of the cable trains; overhead was the thunderous noise of the Elevated. It was all like a huge cauldron of noise and dangers. Dick declared to himself that it was the modern Inferno. And yet, as he passed toward the station of the Elevated with Wooton, Dick began to understand something of the fascination that the place, even in its most noisome aspects, was able to exert. In the very rush and roar, in the ceaseless hum and murmur and groaning, there was epitomized the eager fever of life, its joys and its pains. Here, after all, was life. And it was life that Dick had come to taste.

There was a quick ride on the Elevated, Dick catching various glimpses of unsightly buildings that showed their undress uniform, of dim-lit back rooms where one caught hints of dismal poverty, of roofs that seemed to shudder under the banner of dirty clothes fluttering in the breeze. The town seemed, from this view, like the slattern who is all radiant at night, at the ball, but who, next morning, is an unkempt, untidy hag.

Mrs. Annie McCallum Stewart rose rather languidly as they were announced. Dick noticed that in some mysterious way she managed to give a peculiar grace to almost her every movement; there was something of a tigress in the way she walked. She gave her hand to Wooton—"Delightful of you to come so soon," she murmured.

"One of the things I live for, my dear Mrs. Stewart," said Wooton, "is to surprise people. Knew you didn't expect me, so I came. Brought a dear friend of mine, Mrs. Stewart, Mr. Lancaster. Want you to like him."

"My only prejudice against you, Mr. Lancaster," was Mrs. Stewart's smiling reply, "is that you come under Mr. Wooton's protection. I pretend I'm immensely fond of him, but I'm not; I'm only afraid of him; he's too clever." And, still laughing at Wooton in such a way as to show the exquisite perfection of her teeth, she presented young Lancaster to several of the others who were sitting about the room, chatting and sipping tea. He had a vague idea of several stiff young men bowing to him, of an equal number of splendidly appareled, but unhandsome girls, looking at him with supercilious nods, and of hearing names that faded as easily as they touched him. He found himself, presently, sitting on a low divan, opposite to a girl with dreamy blue eyes behind pince-nez eyeglasses. He hadn't caught her name; he knew no more of her tastes, of the things she was likely to converse about than did the Man in the Moon. But he instinctively opined that it was necessary to seem rather than to be, to skim rather than to dive.

"I've been 'round the circle," he said, trying a smile, "and I'm delivered up to you. I hope you'll treat me well."

The girl with the blue eyes looked at him a moment in silence. Then she said, abruptly: "This is the first time that you've been down here, isn't it? I knew it! Well, these things are not bad—when you get used to them. Now, you're not used to them. Confess, are you?"

Dick shook his head. "I am innocent as a lamb," he said, with mock apology.

The girl went on: "Well, that may do as a novelty. Annie's great on new blood, you know. Shouldn't wonder if she took you up. How are you on theosophy?"

Dick stared. What sort of a torrent of curiosity was this that was gushing forth from this peculiar creature? "To tell you the truth," he hazarded, "I am not 'on' at all."

She smiled. "Ah, that's bad. However, I dare say there's something else. Now, how are you on art?"

"I know a little something." He smiled to himself, wondering how much of the actual practical knowledge of art there was in all that room, outside of what he himself possessed.

"Ah, a little something. Well, that's all that's needed, nowadays. The great point is to know 'a little something' about everything. To know anything thoroughly is to be a bore. A man of that sort is always didactic on the one subject he is familiar with, and absolutely stupid on all other things. However, what's the use of considering those people? They're quite impossible." She began tapping the carpet with her slipper. "Speaking of impossible people," she went on, "there's Mrs. Tremont. Over there with the grey waist. Intellectually, she's impossible; socially she is the possible in essence. She was a Miss Alexander, of Virginia; then she married Tremont, and lived in Boston long enough to get Boston superciliousness added to the natural haughtiness given to her in her birth. She talks pedigree, and dreams of precedence. She goes everywhere, and I fancy she thinks that when she hands St. Peter her card that personage will bow in deference and announce her name in particularly awestruck tones. The girl who is talking to the tall man with the military mustache is Miss Tremont. She is her mother, plus the world and the devil."

Dick interrupted her, as she paused to sip her tea. "Yes," he said, "and now tell me who you are?"

She lifted her eyebrows a trifle. "You have audacity," she said, "and I begin to think you are clever.

42

Audacity is successful only when one is clever. When one is stupid, audacity is a crime. Who am I? Well—" she smiled again at the thought of his assurance. "Why not ask my enemies? But you don't know who is my enemy, who is my friend. Well, I am the Philistine in this circle of the elect. I'm a cousin of Mrs. Stewart's, and I come because I am fond of being amused. She herself amuses me most. She seems to be so tremendously in earnest, and she's so unfathomably insincere. She hates me, you know, because I didn't marry John Stewart when he proposed to me. Then, I never did anything, or had a fad, or was eccentric, so I don't really belong here; but, as I said before, the house amuses me, and I come. I don't know why I tell you this, but I don't care very much, and besides, I believe you're still genuine. It's so pathetic to be genuine; it reminds me of a baby rabbit—blind eyes and fuzz. I'm not sure, but it's my idea, that if you want to keep Mrs. Stewart's good graces you'll have to do nothing harder than stay genuine. It's so novel. Most of us, today, couldn't be genuine again any more than we could be born again. Ah, here's my dear cousin approaching. I suppose she comes to rescue you from my clutches. If you want to please her immensely, tell her I bored you to death. She'll have the thought for desert all week."

Mrs. Stewart sailed toward them with a queenly sweep that was decidedly imposing. She had decided to have a chat with young Lancaster. When she had seen him in the office of the *Torch*, and now, when he first entered the room, she had seen at a glance that he was handsome enough not to need cleverness; but she was curious to see whether he would interest her in other than visual ways. "You've been most fortunate," she said to Dick, as she reached them, "with Miss Leigh to interpret us for you. Has she told you, I wonder, that she is my favorite cousin? But now, I want to talk to you about art. If Miss Leigh will surrender you to me—?"

"I've been talking to Mr. Wooton about you," she said as she bore him away in triumph, "and he tells me you've only been in town for a few weeks. You still have vivid impressions, I suppose. When one has lived here for years and years, one's impressionability gets hardened. It takes something very forcible to really rouse us. And even then we prefer to let some one of us experience the sensation; it is so much easier to take another's word for it, and follow in the rut. That is how most of our present day fads come about. Some one gets pierced between the casings of the armour of indifference, and the rest of us take the cue and join in the chorus of ecstasy. We don't go to hear Patti or Paderewski, you know, because, we really feel their art deeply; it is because someone once felt it and it became the fashion." While she talked, she had led him into a window-nook and motioned

him to a fauteuil that covered the cres-
cent-shaped niche. As she sat down,
the lines of her figure could be traced
through the perfect fit of her gown.
He noticed what finish, what art there
was about the picture she made as she
sat there, beside him. Her gown was a
delicate shade of gray; the crepe seemed
to love her as a vine loves a tree, so
closely did it follow and cling to the
lines of her hips, her waist, her
shoulders. Over her sleeves, immensely wide, as the fashion of the time
decreed, fell lapels of silk. She had on
low shoes, and above them he could see
the neat contour of her ankles, also
clad in gray. "However," she went
on, "I did not intend to talk of the
fashion; I wanted to ask you how the
town struck your artistic side. Don't
you find as great pictures in a street
full of life as in a valley full of shadow?
Isn't there more of the history of today
in the faces of the people you meet on
the Avenue than in a stretch of blue
sky, a white sail, and a background of
Venice?"

"I see you're something of a realist?"

"Don't! Please don't That word
gets on my nerves. I suppose my
amiable cousin, Miss Leigh, told you
we were all blue-stockings, and dilettan-
tes. I assure you we've got beyond the
Realism *versus* Romance stage of
disputation. Really, you don't know
how you disappointed me with that
question. Mr. Wooton told me you
were original!"

Dick flushed a little. "He also told

me," he retorted, "that you were extraordinary. I begin to believe him." His tone had a suspicion of pique in it. But Mrs. Stewart beamed.

"Ah," she said, "I like you when you look like that. That's—h'm, now what is that?—anger, I suppose? It's really so long since I had a real emotion that I don't know how it's done. Do you know, I think you and I are going to be great friends! Yes, I feel I'm going to like you immensely. Won't you try to like me?" She leaned over toward him, and his shy young eyes caught the faint flutter of lace on her breast with something of dim bewilderment. Her lips were parted, and her teeth shone like twin rows of pearls. She went on, before he had time to do more than begin a stammer of embarassment, "Yes, just as long as you stay real, and genuine, I want you to come and see me very often; as often as you possibly can. I imagine that talking to you is going to be like dipping in the fountain of youth. Tell me, you people out there in the country, how do you keep so young?"

"Ask me that, Mrs. Stewart, when I have found out how it is that you in town lose your youth so soon."

"True. You will be the better judge. But you never told me how it strikes the artist in you, this town of ours."

"I haven't had time to think yet how it strikes me. I'm busy finding out all about it. Just at present it's all like the genius that came from the fisherman's vessel in the Arabian Nights: it is a huge coil of smoke that stifles me with its might and its thickness. I know there are wonderful color-effects all about me, but my nerves are still so eager for the mere taste of it all that I can't digest anything. Besides—" he stopped and sighed a little—"I must not begin to think of paint for years. I'm a mere apprentice. I just scratch and rub, and scratch and rub, as a brother artist puts it."

"But one sees some very pretty effects in black-and-white. Look at *Life*, for instance—"

"No, Mrs. Stewart, if you would be loyal to me, don't look at the aforesaid 'loathsome contemporary,' as they say out West." It was Wooton who had approached, and interrupted Mrs. Stewart with an easy nonchalance that, in almost any other man, would have been an unpardonable rudeness. He threw himself on a chair and continued: "Mrs. Stewart, you have wounded me sorely. I bring you a disciple and what do you do? You buttonhole him, as it were, and preach treason to him. For, you must confess, that to tell people to look at *Life* when they might be looking at— h'm—another periodical, whose name I reverence too highly to mention before a traitoress, is High Treason."

For reply, Mrs. Stewart tapped Wooton lightly on the lips with a large ivory paper-cutter that she had been toying with. "As I was saying, when rudely interrupted, look at—"

"My dear Mrs. Stewart, why this feverish desire to look at life? I ask you

both, is life pretty? Remember M. Zola
and Mr. Howells. They are supposed
to give us life, are they not? Well, the
one flushes a sewer, and the other hands
us weak tea. I prefer not to contem-
plate life. I am obliged to read the
morning papers because it is become
necessary to know today the unpleasantness that happened yesterday. But
otherwise I assure you that life—"

This time, Mrs. Stewart tapped him
quite smartly with the paper-cutter.

"You know very well that puns have
been out of fashion for more years than
you have been of age. We were talking
about art, and incidentally about a paper
that encourages art, and you begin a
dissertation on life! What do you
mean?"

Wooton mockingly stifled an effort to
yawn. "As if I ever, by the vaguest
chance, meant anything! I hate to be
asked what I mean. If I knew, I would
probably not tell, and if I do not know
why should I lie? The safest course in
this world is never to mean anything and
to say everything. If I had my life tc
live over again—"

Mrs. Stewart looked at him with a
shudder, lifting her shoulders, while her
mouth showed a smile. "Why speak of
anything so unpleasant?"

"Ah, had you there, Wooton, eh!"
It was Vanstruther, who had strolled
over to pay his respects to Mrs. Stewart.
She held out a hand; he pressed it
lightly. He nodded to Lancaster, and
then looked through the half-drawn
portiers to where in the black-and-gold

48

drawing-room the others were sitting and standing in colorful groups. Some-one was at the piano playing a mazurka of Chopin's. There was a faint click of cups touching saucers; the high notes of the women and the low drawl of the men. Vanstruther looked at them all slowly, and then turned to Mrs. Stewart again. "All in?" he inquired.

Mrs. Stewart nodded and smiled.

"I've not been at your house for so long," Vanstruther continued, "that I'm a little out of the running. Several people here that are new to me. Now, that girl in black?"

"Talking to young Hexam? That's Madge Winters. You remember young Winters who was runner-up in the tennis tournament last season?—sister of his. She's just back from Japan. Has some idea of doing a sort of Edmund Russell gospel of the beautiful *a la* Japan course of readings. Her brother amused me once and I'm going to do what I can for her. Now, who else is there? Let me see: I don't think you ever met Miss Farcreigh before—she's talking to the man at the piano. Delightful girl—her father's the big Standard Oil man, you know—and collects china. Sings a little, too. But chiefly I like her be-cause she's pretty and a great catch. There's a German prince madly in love with her, but her father objects to him because his majesty never did a stroke of work in his life. I believe you know all the others."

"Thank you, yes." Vanstruther turned to Dick and said to him, with a

smile at Mrs. Stewart, "You may find
eccentric people here, Lancaster, but
you will never find unpleasant ones."

"That's where Mrs. Stewart makes
the inevitable mistake," drawled Wooton. "There should be one or two unpleasant ones, merely for the sake of
the others. If it were not for the unpleasant people in the world, it would
hardly be worth while being the other
kind."

"You're as unpleasant as need be,"
was Mrs. Stewart's reply.

"Delighted!" murmured Wooton.
"To have done a duty is always a delight. I have done several. I have
brought you a new disciple, I have leav-
ened your heaven with intrusion of myself, and now—now I must really go.
My virtues are still like incense in my
nostrils. Allow me to waft myself gently
away before they grow rank and stale."

Dick rose at the same moment.
"Oh," Wooton said to him, "you're not
obliged to go yet. Stay and let Mrs.
Stewart enchant you with the nectar of
proximity! I've got to be down at the
Midwinter dance tonight, so I must be
off now."

But Dick, in spite of the other's pro-
testations, insisted that he must really
go also. He assured Mrs. Stewart that
he had enjoyed himself immensely,
promised to come soon and often, and
was presently whirling down-town again
with Wooton. The latter had bought
an evening paper and was carefully pe-
rusing the sporting columns. Dick closed
his eyes, trying to recall the picture he

had just left: the dim-lit drawing-room, with its well-dressed, graceful people; Mrs. Stewart's fascinating voice and figure; the flippant frivolity of all their discourse; the useless sham of all their isms and fads; the clever ease with which everything seemed to be taken for granted, and nothing was ever truly analyzed—how like a phantasmagoria of repellant things it all was, and yet how fascinating! Everyone appeared to know everything; no surprise was ever expressed; no emotion was ever visible. It was fully expected that everyone was possessed of no real aim in life save the riding of a hobby; it was agreed that to appear ignorant of anything was to be vulgar. And yet, in that circle, Dick was hailed as "so delightfully genuine," and was told that he would stand high at court as long as he remained so! Surely these were strange days, and stranger ways! That phrase of Mrs. Stewart's about young Winters grated harshly, too—"He amused me once!"

Was life merely an effort at being forever amused?

Almost, it seemed so.

CHAPTER IV

THE room was dim with smoke. Through the faint veil that curled incessantly toward the ceiling the pictures on the wall took on a misty haze that heightened rather than spoilt their effect. It was not a large room, but the walls were covered with pictures of every sort. It was impossible to escape observing the artistic carelessness that had prevailed in the arrangement of the furniture. Bookcases lined the lower portion of each wall; then came pictures. There was an original by Blum; a marvelously executed facsimile of a black-and-white by Abbey; a Vierge, and a Myrbach. Not the least remarkable 'eature of these ornaments was the manner of their framing. A Parisienne, by Jules Cheret, for instance, all skirts and chic, looked as if she had just burst through the confines of a prison-wall of a daily paper. The carelessly serrated edges, then the white matting, and the brown frame gave a whole that was worth looking at twice. An etching—one of Beardsley's fantasies—was framed all in black; it was more effective than the original.

Over the mantel were scattered photographs of stage divinities in profusion. Many of them had autographs scrawled across the face of the picture. In a niche in the wall a human skull, with a clay pipe stuck jauntily between the teeth, looked out over the smoke.

From the next room, beyond the open portieres, came the sound of a violin and a piano.

The air of Mascagni's "Intermezzo" died away, and for it was substituted a slow dirge-like melody. Belden, in the front room, broke out into an explosive, "Ah, that's the stuff! Everybody sing: 'For they're hangin' Danny Deever in the mohn-nin'.'" The wail of that solemn ballad went echoing through the house, all the men present joining in. Belden, who had been lying at full length on the floor, explaining the beauties of a charcoal drawing by Menzel to a group of three other artists — Marsboro, of the *Telegraph*, Evans, of the *Standard*, and a younger man, Stevely, who was still going to the Art School—had jumped to his feet and was slowly waving a pencil in mock leadership of a chorus. Vanstruther, who was stealing an evening from society for Bohemia's sake, was far back in a huge rocking chair; a fantastic work by Octave Uzanne on his knee, and his legs stretched out over the center table; he now held his pipe in his hand and hummed the refrain in a deep bass.

"Go on," urged Belden, as the last notes moaned themselves away in the smoke, "go on, give us something else!" But Stanley laid his violin down on a bookcase and declared that his arm was tired.

Vanstruther pulled at his pipe again, until he was sure he still had fire. Then he declared, oracularly, "Stanley, you look tremendously religious to-night. Been jilted?

"No, shaved. You confirm an impression I have that a man never feels so religious as when he has just been shaved. I assure you that in this way I could really read one of your 'shockers,' Van, and feel that I was doing my duty."

"Oh," Belden cut in, going over to

one of the bookcases, "anything to stop Stanley from hearing himself talk. It makes him drunk. Seeing we had a ballad of Kipling's just now, suppose some one reads something of his. Then someone else can sit still, and think of his sins, while the pen-and-ink men make sketches of him. How'll that do, eh?

"All right." It was Vanstruther, whose voice came from over the smoke. "I'll read if you like; and Stanley can get a far-away expression into his countenance, while you other fellows put his ephemeral beauty on paper. What'll it be?"

Stanley, who was rolling himself onto a sofa in the corner, murmured, while he rolled a cigarette with a deft motion of his fingers, "Oh, give us that yarn about the things in a dead man's eye, what's the title again—'At the End of the Passage', isn't it? I'm in the mood for something of that pleasant sort. By the way, aren't we a man shy, Belden?"

"Yes. Young Lancaster hasn't arrived yet. I had a great time getting him to say he would come; he has scruples about Sunday, and all that sort of thing; but he'll turn up pretty soon, I know. Here's the book, Van." He handed the volume across the table. Stanley, after a few chaffing remarks had passed back and forth, was arranged into a position that would give the artists a sharp profile to work from. The artists began sharpening pencils, and pinning paper on drawing boards.

And then, for a time, there was nothing but the sounds of pens and pencils going over paper, and Vanstruther's voice reading that story of Indian heat and hopelessness. In the other room McRoy, the man who had been playing Stanley's piano accompaniment, was reading Swinburne to himself.

The bell rang suddenly. Belden threw his sketch down and opened the door. "Lancaster, I suppose," he said. Then they heard his voice in the hall, greeting the newcomer, who was presently ushered in and airily made known to such of the men as he had not yet been introduced to.

"You've just missed a treat, my boy," said Belden, pushing Dick into a chair. "Vanstruther has been reading us a yarn of Kipling's. You're fond of Kip., I suppose?"

While Dick said, "Oh, yes, indeed," Stanley put in.

"It's lucky for you you are, because Belden here swears by the trinity of Kipling, Riley and Henri Murger. He has occasional flirtations with other authors, but he generally comes back to those three. But then, when you get to know Belden better, you will realize that he has what is technically known as 'rats in his garret.' Do you know what he once did, just to illustrate? Walked miles in a bleak country district that he might reach a certain half-disabled bridge and there sit, reading De Quincey's 'Vision of Sudden Death' by moonlight! The man who can do that can do anything that's weird."

"There's only one way to stop your tongue, Stanley," Belden remarked humoredly, "and that is to ask you to play for us again. Lancaster has never heard you yet, you know."

Stanley looked out into the other room. "What do you say, Mac? Shall we tune our harps again?"

"Just as cheap," said the other, without looking up from his book.

They began to play. From Raff's "Cavatina," they strayed into a melody by Rubinstein; then it was a wild gallop through comic operas, popular songs, and Bowery catches. While they played the men in the other room began comparing sketches. Vanstruther ushered Dick into many of the artistic treasure-holds that the room contained. Also, he supplied him with running comments on some of the things they saw all about them. Dick, though he scarcely felt at ease, felt strongly the fascination of all this devil-may-care atmosphere. The haze of smoke; the melodious airs from beyond the portieres; the careless attire and jaunty nonchalance of the men, all drew him with a sort of sensual hypnotism, even while his inner being felt that he himself was a little better than this. He was in the land of Don't-Care; dogmas, creeds, faiths had no place here; everything was "do as you please, and let your neighbor please himself." He said but little; he thought a great deal.

One of the artists called Vanstruther over to the open bookcase, to show him a sketch by Gibson. Dick looked about him, picked up a copy of Omar Khayyam, that had Vedder's illustrations, and buried himself in the gentle philosophy of that classic.

But Belden was again become restless. Mere melody never did anything but irritate him. "Oh, play some nigger music," he asked. Then, when a few merry jingles from "'Way down South" had played themselves in and out of the echoes, Stanley put his violin down with a decisive gesture. "There, I've paid my way, I think!" When the piano had been closed, and the violin laid away in its case, he went on, " 'Seems to me it's about time you were bringing along your friend Murger?"

Belden walked toward the shelf where the "Scenes de la Vie de Boheme" had its place. As he took it out, however, he said, "Come to think of it, Marsboro's going to commit matrimony pretty soon, I hear. Any objections?" He held the volume in the air, questioningly.

Marsboro laughed, and shook his head. "No, no," he said, "go on!"

"Just as if," Stanley observed, "a man about to be married knew what objections were! Dante Gabriel Belden, in some things you are weirdly primitive."

"I would sooner be primitive than effete," was Belden's retort.

Stanley turned to Marsboro. "Don't think me curious, old man, but is it any girl I know?"

Before Marsboro could reply, Vanstruther broke in with, "I'll bet money it's not! You don't suppose Marsboro

is likely to think of marrying a woman
with a past!"

Marsboro flushed a little; and moved
uneasily in his chair. Dick, looking up
from his Omar Khayam, wondered
how the man could endure such verbal
pitch and toss with such a subject.

But Stanley turned away from the
matter with a sneer. "My dear fellow," he said, "if it will soothe your
sweet soul, I am quite willing to admit
that in the course of my life I have
known some women who had pasts.
They are invariably interesting. The
only difference between a woman with
a past and a man of the same sort is
that the man still has a future before
him. And a man with a future is as
pathetic as a little boy chasing a butterfly: even if he wins the game, there is
nothing but a corpse, and some dust on
his fingers."

Belden, turning the pages of the
Murger, said, deprecatingly, "Don't
get Stanley started on moral reflections:
in the first place, they are not moral;
in the second place they reflect nothing
but his own perverted soul. Talking
morals with some men is like turning
the pages of an edition de luxe with
inky fingers."

Stanley laughed. "Good boy! But
now go on with Rodolph and his flirtations. Where did you leave off? Hadn't
he just written some poetry, spent the
proceeds on feasting his friends, and
the night in a tree?"

Belden began to read.

In spite of himself, Dick began to

58

feel the fascination of Murger's recital of all those rollicking, roystering episodes in the Latin Quarter. He let the Omar fall idly into his lap, and gave himself up to listening to Belden's reading. The other men smoked and smiled. Dick's sense of humor told him that there was something quaint in the way Belden intentionally fed his own love for Bohemianism with another's description; none the less he admitted that there was no sham, dilettante Bohemianism about this place and the men present. It was not the Bohemianism of claw-hammer coats and high-priced champagne; of little suppers, after the theater, in a black and gold boudoir, where the women tasted some Welsh rarebit and declared that they were afraid it was "awfully Bohemian, don't you know!" It was the Bohemia that recked naught of others, but had as banner, "Do as you please," and as watchword "Don't care." It was the old philosophy of Epicurus brought to modern usage.

The good-humored account that Henri Murger gave of so many picturesque light-love escapades, that had so much of pathos mingled with their unmorality, began to find in Dick a vein of sympathy. He felt that it was all very pleasant; all was charmingly put; it was interesting.

"There," Belden declared, as he finished reading the episode of the flowers that Musette watered every night, because she had promised to love while those blossoms lived, "I'm dry, that's what I am. I think it's about time we investigated. Come on into the kitchen, people. There's some coffee and cake and fruit. Shouldn't wonder if you could find a bottle or two of beer on the ice, too."

They trooped out, through a room and corridor, to the kitchen. There was a bare, deal table, a cooking range, a gas stove, a refrigerator and several doors leading to closets. Every man brought his own chair. A search was begun for cups, plates, knives and forks. Each man sat down where he pleased. The coffee that was made was hardly such as one gets at Tortoni's, but it was refreshing, nevertheless. The sound of corks drawing from beer-bottles, of knives rattling on plates, and of indiscriminate, lusty chatter filled the place. Belden was the master-spirit. He saw that everyone helped himself; he chaffed and he laughed; he looked after the provender and the cigars. The infection of all this jollity touched Dick; he began to say to himself that to worry himself with conscientious scruples just because it was on a Sunday instead of a Monday that all this happened, was to be something of a prig. And he had always had a decided aversion to being that particular sort of nuisance. He resigned himself completely to the spirit of the time and place.

McRoy broke into the babel of talk with a plaintive, "Everybody listen for about a minute, will you? I want to ask Belden a solemn question: Belden,

have you finished that copy of 'Old-
World Idyls' that you were going to
illustrate for me in pen-and-ink, on the
margins?"

Belden smiled. "Why, to tell you
the truth, old man—" he began, but the
other interrupted him with, "There!
publicly branded! Belden, you're the
awfulest breaker of oaths that ever was
let live. You've had the book six
months, and I'll bet you've never drawn a
stroke on it!"

"The mistake you made," put in Stanley, "was to believe that he ever *would*
do the thing. He once made a promise
of that sort to me, but that was so long
ago that I think I'm another person
now."

"If the theory of evolution is correct,"
said Vanstruther, "your late lamented
self must have been and abominably
corrupt person."

Stanley sighed, "Perhaps so. I am
trying, you know, day by day, to approach the sublime pinnacle on which
you, my dear Van, tower above the rest
of mankind. However—" he reached
his arm out over the table—"Any beer
left over there?"

Belden handed a mug and a bottle
over to him.

"By the way," cut in Marsborc, "ever
had any more trouble with the neighbors here? Said you kept them awake
Sunday nights with your unholy orgies,
didn't they?"

"Yes. But I said if they were going
to kick on that score I would get out an
injunction against that girl of theirs that

is always trying to play 'After the Ball,' with one hand. So I fancy our lances are both at rest."

So, with much careless clatter, and exchange of banter, they ate and drank lustily until their hunger was appeased. Then, pushing their plates and mugs into the middle of the table they leaned back to enjoy the pleasures of the god Nicotine. And presently someone hinted that the empty plates and the litter of the late-lamentedness in general was not a cheering sight and they might as well proceed into the studio again. There was a shoving back of chairs, a trooping through the corridor, and they were all assembled once more in the front rooms. Mc-Roy hid himself behind a book. The others grouped themselves around the piano. The plaintiff strains of Chevalier's "The Future Mrs. 'Awkins" filled the room, born aloft on the impetus of five pairs of lungs.

There was a violent ringing at the outer bell. It was some little time before the men at the piano heard the din; it was only at McRoy's muttered "Somebody's pulling your front door bell off the wires, Belden!" that the latter went to open. The men in the room could hear the sound of a man's voice, a quick passage of sentences, then good-nights, all vaguely, over the strains of the coster-ditty.

"What do you think," said Belden, coming in again, "has happened? It was Ditton, of the *Telegraph*—lives a door or two north—just dropped in to tell me a bit of news that he thought would interest me. Wooton of the 'Torch' has disappeared, leaving the property deeply in debt. Nobody knows where he is. Jove, come to think of it, that's pretty rough news for you, Lancaster!"

"Yes," said Lancaster, "it is. And yet there is one consolation, he paid me within a week of what was due me."

There was a cessation of all other discussion to make room for the consideration of this bit of news. Everybody agreed that it was too bad that so good a sheet as the "Torch" should go the way of the majority. Concerning Wooton the opinions differed. Belden began to apologize to Lancaster for having led him into this "mess," as he called it, while Stanley sneered at everybody for not having seen through Wooton long ago.

"He is inordinately vain," said Stanley, "and frightfully extravagant. Clever. Lazy—awfully lazy. He can sit back in his chair and tell you how to run the New York *Herald*, and he has been able to get nothing profitable into or out of his paper from the time he began until now. He theorizes beautifully; the only thing he can really do successfully is to borrow money and talk to women. He used to amuse me just in the way an actor amuses me. Half the time I think he was deceiving even himself. I always thought he would do this very thing, one of these days. He used to have what old women call 'spells' now and

again, when he found himself hard up
for cash, that were really the most
curious performances. He would stay
away from his office altogether; genius
as he was in warding off collectors,
he used to prefer not to face them
sometimes. There was—I should say
there is—a woman, one of the cleverest,
most cultured woman in town, who
was fond of him in an elderly-sister
sort of way, and he used to go to her
and borrow money. Think of it:
borrow money from a woman! She
saw through him long ago, I know,
and yet he used to use such artifice—
such tears, and promises of better-
ment as the men employed!—that she
always helped him in the end. Then
he gambled to try to make the big
stake that would enable him to run a
rich man's paper; the only result is
that he got deeper and deeper into
the hole. All the time he avoided
his office; if he scraped up a banknote
or two he would send them along, per
messenger boy, to the foreman of the
composing-room and have the printers
paid, at least. You must pay the printers
and the pressmen, you know, even if
you let a lot of literary devils starve!
And then some guardian angel would
send along a college chum, or some
fellow with more loyality than discre-
tion, and A. B. Wooton would make a
big 'borrow' and be once more the
genial, cynical man-of-the-world that
the rest of you know. This time I
presume the angel refused to come.

The end had to come; it was simply a huge game of 'bluff.'"

"How is it you know all this?" asked one of the others.

"My dear fellow," was Stanley's answer, "I have *gambled* with him. All through one of those periods when he was engaged, ostrich-like, in sticking his head into the sand, I was with him. Besides, I know something of his private affairs. He had sunk all of his own money long ago; for the last year or so the *Torch* and Wooton have been living on the gullibility of others. It seems strange that this should be possible in this smart American city, but Wooton was not an ordinary bluffer; he was a genius. Owing you hundreds of dollars he could talk to you all day so skilfully on the one especial vanity of your heart that you would feel much more like offering him another hundred than like even so much as mentioning the old debt. I feel sorry for him. He should have a patron, to humor him in all his extravagances; he would be splendid, splendid!"

But Lancaster, whom the news had touched a good deal, declared that it was time he was taking himself off. Belden accompanied him to the door, and spoke to him encouragingly about another position that he thought Dick could easily obtain. Then Lancaster passed out into the night.

CHAPTER V

CARRIAGES lined the sidewalk for blocks in every direction. There was a slight sprinkle of rain falling, and the shining rubber coats and hats of the coachmen caught the electric light in fantastic streaks. Horses were stamping, and chafing the bit. From every direction came a stream of humanity, all making for the Auditorium. Carriages were arriving every moment; the bystanders and ticket scalpers caught glimpses of light hose and dainty opera shoes and skirts that were lifted for an instant. Men in black capes were hurrying about busily. The cable cars emptied load after load of well-dressed men and women. All the world and his wife was going to the opera.

Dick Lancaster, as he got out of his hansom, looked appreciatively at the picture that all this hurrying throng made, and shaking some of the rain drops off his coat, entered the opera house. As he looked about him at the richly caparisoned human animals all on pleasure bent, at the nonchalance that the mirrors told him he himself was displaying, it came over him with something of amusement that there had been decided changes in Richard Lancaster since that young person first came to town. Impressionable as wax, the town had already cast its fascinations over him; he was in the charmed circle. He had been put up at one of the best of the clubs; he had been made much of, socially, by the select set that allowed

the preferences of Mrs. Annie McCallum
Stewart to dictate the distinction between the Somebodies and the Nobodies;
he had been successful enough, pro-
fessionally, to enable him to move in the
world as befitted his tastes. It is to be
confessed that his tastes, now that they
had been whetted by the approach of
opportunities, were not of the most
economical. He was fond of all things
that show the intellectual aristocrat; he
liked to look well, to dine well, to talk
well, and to enjoy good music. He
liked the comfort, the remoteness from
the mere vagaries of the weather, that
this town life afforded. Here was a night
such as in the country would be dismal
unspeakably; yet nothing but brilliance
and enjoyment was evident in his present surroundings.

He threw his shoulders back with
something of proud pleasure in his own
well-being, as he handed his cape and
opera-hat to the caretaker. Yes, life
was good! It tasted well, and he was
young, and there would yet be many
long, delicious draughts of it!

Mrs. Stewart was in her box. Several
girls, whose low-cut dresses seemed to be
longing for something more worth showing, were seated on the chairs that surrounded the central figure, Mrs. Stewart.
In the background of this, as of all other
boxes, was a phalanx of white shirt-
fronts. It looked like the fore-front of
an attacking army; first the flash of
bayonets, as they are to be found in
woman's eyes, and then the heavier
artillery, the stolid force of masculinity.

In the wide corridors behind the boxes, in the foyers, and up and down the marble stairways, the stream of people flowed back and forth. Presently the conductor of the orchestra took his seat. There was a hastening toward seats and boxes, and the overture of the "Cavalleria Rusticana" floated out in echoes.

Young Lancaster reached the Stewart box just as the first bars were streaming forth. Mrs. Stewart leaned her head gracefully back over her right shoulder, and smiled up at him. She stretched up a beautifully gloved hand, and whispered a "Glad you came through the rain, after all. Awfully disappointed if you hadn't!" at him. He nodded to the other women, and shook hands with Mr. Stewart and some of the other members of the white-shirted, blank-faced phalanx.

"Ah," whispered Mrs. Stewart with a languid show of interest, and putting her lorgnette up, "there is Calve!"

There was a flutter of hand-clappings that went like a light wave from the stalls to the upper balconies. And then began that exquisite, dramatic exposition of rustic jealousy that Mascagni has so wonderfully set to music. As Santuzza, Calve was magnetic. Actress as much as singer she riveted all attention. Her face was the picture of agony the while she was contemplating the inner vision of her betrayal by Turiddu. Then, the jealous hatred flashing out at Lola, her rival; and lastly the self-accusing sorrow that covered her when she saw the effect of her tale-bearing against her former lover. In the interval there was the marvellous Intermezzo. Mrs. Stewart leaned back in her chair and closed her eyes. When it was over she said, "There is something of the world's joy and something of its pain in that melody. It appeals to me wonderfully."

Lancaster put in, "One of the men at the club declared that it was the only thing that had given him real emotion for—oh, years."

"He must have been a very blase creature," said one of the other women.

"He is," assented Lancaster.

Their further conversation was interruped by the rising of the curtain. When it came down again there was a general movement toward the foyers. Some of the tall and pale young men strolled out to smoke cigars and talk of the boxing match that was going to come off at the club in a day or so. With much fluttering of fans and swishing of skirts the angular girls betook themselves from Mrs. Stewart's box to see if they "could see any of the other girls." Mrs. Stewart and Dick Lancaster were left in sole possession. He took a chair beside her and looked over into the stalls.

"Only fair," she said, noting his visual measurement of the size of the audience.

"Yes. These people don't want the New. They want 'Faust' and 'Aida,' and they think 'Tannhauser' is the very last in music. It will be years before they see the gem-like beauty of this new Italian school."

"And yet—it's a return to the old."

"That is why. The old things are the best, if you only go far enough into the past.' We are never really modern, we are merely old in a new way."

"Do you know—" she leaned her white elbow on the cushioned chair-back and placed her forefinger just under her ear, so that from the elbow up her arm formed a white, beautiful rest for the attractive face, and looking young Lancaster smilingly in the eyes, tapped her foot caressingly to the floor — "do you know that I think I shall have to cut you off my list very soon? You have —h'm—changed a great deal in the few months I have known you. You occasionally make speeches that sound almost cynical. You were always clever; you always talked brightly, but you never used to believe some of the sharp things you said; now I think you are beginning to. I liked you because you were different; you are not different any more, at least not different in the same way. You will never be as stupid as most of the others; but I am afraid, too, that you will never be quite as genuine as you were."

He sighed as he looked at her. He smiled very faintly as he answered, "Yes, I am afraid you are right. I am not as I was." His gaze swept out over the stalls, the crowded foyer, the brilliance everywhere. "But how could I have done anything else than let all this affect me a little? I am pliable, I suppose, and I bend easily to the wind. I came here to taste life. As soon as I began to sip the cup I found that I was going to like it immensely. I trod the way of the world that I might see what manner of men walk there, and what sort of a road it was. Presently, I found that I liked that path so much that I preferred it to the bypaths of solitude and asceticism. And what has it mattered as long as I have not neglected the work there is for me to do? No one can say I have changed in that respect. I work harder than ever. It's not fair of you to upbraid me. A great deal of it is your own doing."

"Yes?"

"Of course it is. You have been my pilot out of the land of the Narrows. When I came up here I was narrow. I thought about things dogmatically, and applied hard and fast rules to every sort of conduct. Now I am broader. I know that where the world moves at lightning speed you cannot apply the same tenets that hold good in a village where life is lived at a cripple's gait and where routine is the reigning deity."

"You would not have called it a 'cripple's gait' a little while ago," interposed Mrs. Stewart.

He flushed slightly but went on: "I realize now that since we have but one life to live, we should live it as fully as we may. I could not have seen the life that all of you here are living without realizing that it was a fuller life than the one the country afforded me. So, cost what it may, I must needs live it also."

She looked at him curiously. "Yes,"

she repeated, half to him and half to herself, "cost what it may."

"Besides," he went on, looking away
from her, and with something of regret
in his voice," I have grown worldly because I loved a worldly woman. You--
you have made me love you."

She lifted her eyebrows a trifle, turned
her head, with the eyelids drawn down
over her eyes, toward him, and opened the
lids slowly, with a smile on her lips.
Then she looked past him to where her
husband was leaning over a chair in one
of the other boxes.

"Don't you think John is looking very
handsome tonight?" she asked softly.

Lancaster, who had gone red and pale
in waves, answered, through set lips,
"Very."

Then the curtain went up on "Pagli-
acci."

It was the first time that Lancaster
had heard Leoncavallo's opera. In its
novel charm his shame and mortification
—shame at having spoken those words
to Mrs. Stewart and mortification at the
rebuff they had only naturally brought
him—were for the time being swallowed
up. With eager eyes and attentive ears
he watched and listened to the play within the play. First the arrival of the
mountebanks. Amid the laughs and re-
joicings of the villagers the theater-
tent is set. Then the effort of the clown
to make love to Canio's wife; the slash
of the whip from her, the muttered
curses from him. But the woman is

fickle, after all; the villager, Silvio, is more successful than the clown was. The sudden approach of Canio, the husband, led hither by the vengeful clown, still smarting under the whip; the escape of Silvio, and the woman's refusal to tell the name of her lover. And so, to the wonderful second act, where tragedy is so dexterously woven into comedy; where, under the guise of a drama that the mountebanks proffer the villagers on their little stage, the greater drama of Canio's jealousy is spun out to its tragic ending. In between the lines of the dialogue intended for the village audience come lines wrung from Canio's heart that sear their way into his wife's breast, spite of her stage-smiles and graces. And when, at the last, Canio, in his baffled rage, would strike her, and Silvio, her lover, rushes from the audience in rescue, only to be stabbed by the finally exultant husband, young Lancaster involuntarily shuddered. There was something griping in the wonderful display of human rage and jealousy that this young tenor gave in Canio; in the final words, full of tragic, double, ironical meaning, "La comedie e finitn!" there was something of a sentence of death. And somehow, in Silvio there seemed to be something of himself: that lover's terrible fate was fraught for him, in the conscience-stricken state he found himself in, with warning and protest. While the applause, reaching curtain-call after curtain-call, surged all about him, young Lancaster was lost in reverie. He was changed, yes.

He had adapted himself to the manners of the town; but he still had a most nervous conscience, sharp, unblunted. He sat still, with his chin hiding his upper shirt stud.

Mrs. Stewart's voice roused him. Her husband was already engaged in putting her cloak about her shoulders. "Wonderful, wasn't it?" she said sweetly. "We shall see you Wednesday, shall we not?"

He bowed and stammered something, he hardly knew what.

The opera was over.

That night, before he took off his dress clothes, Dick sat down and wrote to his mother. It was a thing he had not been so steadfast in of late as once he had been.

In one place he wrote: "You ask me, mother mine, how I like the town now that it is no longer strange to me. Oh, I like it only too well. The old place, the old friends, the sweet gentle tenor of all the old life out there in Lincolnville, all seem like some far-off dream to me. My ears and eyes are full of the many sounds and sights of the town; the multifarious vistas, and the ever-changing face of the street. I like the town and yet I fear it. Sometimes its might oppresses me, and I feel as if I wanted to get out in the woods near our home and lie down at full length on the mossy bank, where the creek sings soothingly and the sun hangs like a golden ball in a clear sky. I want to hear the crickets, and the deep silence of the nights, and the echoes of detached laughter floating over the meadows. I want to watch the sunlight as it comes through the leaves and plays hide-and-seek on the lawn; I want to watch the hawk circling in the air, the chickens scurrying fearfully at the sight of him. And then again the feverish itch to be in the very middle of this maelstrom, the town, seizes me. I long for the very thick and foremost of the struggle, and the picture of Lincolnville fades away. At this present time of the year, though, I can really prefer the town without seeming a slave to it.

"It is in the winter, or in the early spring, when country places are chiefly seas of mud and slush that one most deeply realizes the delights of dwelling in town. Modern invention has put the town dweller beyond the weather's jealous bites. We step into a hansom, we drive to the club, we have dinner; behind club doors, and in club comfort we are above all the slings and arrows of the elements; we drive to the theatre, and the black-and-white splendor of our men, as well as the fur-decked rosiness of our women, is only enhanced by contrast against the frowny murkings of the sky. I have noticed that the finale, the curtain-fall of any important public event, such as a dinner, a dance, or an opera, is always a more picturesque thing when the carriages have to drive away through the sleet. Whereas, the country! The weather is the world and all that therein is; you can't get away from it. Mud is king! * * *

"I am doing something in paint now, just to feed this terrible ambition of mine. The pen-and-ink work is all very well, and it does bring the bread and butter, but it is not what I want for ever and ever. And I think I am going to have for my subject just such a scene as I wrote of a moment ago: the moment before the carriages drive away through the rain, with everybody in gala attire and scintillant with brightness and insincerity. For the town is insincere, mother, and cruel. Some day, perhaps I, too, will become insincere. I do not know. I pray it may not be so. But I am alarming you causelessly. I am only a little tired and unnerved tonight. I have been to the opera, and it was just a little affecting. So don't mind what I said just now. * * * * I am getting rather tired and will say good-night. * * * "

CHAPTER VI

IN the early dawn there had been a slight shower of rain, but by the time the sun was high enough to shine over the town's highest buildings, the clouds parted, and presently drifted away altogether, leaving the golden disc full freedom in giving a brilliant look to the clean-washed streets. By noon everything was as bright as a newly-scoured kitchen.

It was at that time of the year when spring is kissing a greeting to summer. There was not too much heat. Growth and activity were not yet subdued by the later lassitude of midsummer. In the parks the trees were full of blossoms, the flowers were spelling out the runes that the gardners had contrived for the Sunday sight-seers, and the roadways were alive with well-equipped traps of every sort. The avenue was colorful and kaleidoscopic. Dog-carts, driven by smartly-gowned, square-sitting girls, bowled along noiselessly, the footmen looking as stolid as if carved in wood. Landaus, with elderly women leaning far back into the cushions, and shading their complexions under lace-decked parasols, went by with an occasional rattling of chains. The careful observer might have noticed that the number of smart vehicles was a trifle larger than usual; there were more coaches out, and the air resounded more often to the various military and hunting-calls that the English grooms were executing on their horns.

It was Derby Day.

Dick was walking along the avenue watching, with his artist eyes open for all the picturesque effect of the whole— the yellow haze of the sun that filled the atmosphere in and out of which all these rapid color-effects flashed swiftly, the thin strip of sky-reflecting water to the east, the line of grass and the sky-touching horizon of huge buildings— when he heard someone calling out his name.

"Lancaster!" It was Stanley, driving a dog-cart and a neat bay cob. "The very man! Jump in, won't you? Going down to the Derby. Thing you should-n't miss; lots of color and all that sort

of thing! Asked Vanstruther to go
down with me, but one of his dime-
novel heroes is ill or something of that
sort, and he's off the list. That's good
of you. Look how you're stepping. This
brute has been eating his head off all
week, and isn't really fit for a Christian
to drive. That's it! Now." They went
spinning along the avenue.

In the instant or two before he climbed
into the dog-cart, Dick had reflected
that while he was not over-fond of
Stanley in a good many ways, the man
was undeniably a clever fellow, always
to be depended on for bright talk; besides he did feel very much like study-
ing the scene of a Derby Day with its
many-colored facets.

Watching the rapid, shifting beauties
of the boulevard, Dick burst into a little
sigh of admiration. "Ah," he said,
"this is good! This is living!"   -

"Youthful enthusiasm," muttered the
other man. "Delightful thing—youthful
enthusiasm—to get over."

"Oh, no! I hope I never shall! What
is life worth if one is not to show that
one enjoys it? How can you look at a
day like this—a splendid, champagne-
like day—and yet—"

"My dear fellow," interrupted Stanley, with a queer smile, "when a man
gets to my time of life there is always
something melancholy to him in the
picture of a spring day. It reminds him
of his own youth: all tears and sunshine.
Today there are neither tears or sunshine; it is all just contemplation. I don't
seem to belong to the play at all, any

more, myself; I'm merely a spectator.
To the spectator there is always something pathetic about joy."

"Your lunch was indigestable, that's
all that is the matter with you," laughed
Dick. "It's a dogma of mine that pessimism is merely another word for indigestion."

"Dogma!" sighed Stanley, "Don't
you know that all dogmas are obsolete?
Don't you know that in this rapid age
we believe everything, accept everything and yet doubt everything?"

"Isn't that a trifle paradoxical?"

"No; only modern! We believe everything that inventors or scientists may
tell us; but in the world spiritual we believe nothing. Is that a paradox?"

"But indigestion is surely, h'm, material rather than spiritual?" Dick enjoyed the verbal parries that he was
always sure of with Stanley. He was
always trying to get at the secret man's
cynicism, a cynicism that was the essence
of what many other men of the world he
lived in seemed to feel, but were not all,
perhaps, so well able to express.

"Oh well," was Stanley's answer, "after
all, it doesn't matter. Nothing makes
any difference." He looked blankly
ahead as if all the world was contained
in the space occupied between the cob's
ears. Then he went on, in his minor
monotone, "No, nothing, except—"

Dick, thinking to be cheery, put in
"Except marriage?"

"No!" came from Stanley, with a
sudden flick of the whip over the cob's
flanks, "that only makes differences."

Dick laughed somewhat impatiently. "Oh!" he urged, "why sit there and be dismal? Why not wake up and live? Surely the air is full of it, of this fair Life? Enjoy it, brace up, be young!"

"Ah, if I only could again, if I only could! Oh, to be young again! He is the Autocrat of today, the young man." He lapsed into his sneer once more. "The young man of today thinks he has the experience of the centuries at his fingertips, whereas he really has only the gloves that were made yesterday and will split tomorrow."

"You are not only unjust," protested Dick, "you are flippant."

"Of course I am! The keynote of this end of the century is lightness. The modern declares that life is but a joke, and a bad one at best. How to live without ever allowing oneself to suspect that life is more than a game in which the odds are heads, Death wins; tails, Man loses: that is the great problem of the decade. The universal solution of the difficulty is the practice of superficiality. Skim! Be light! Never penetrate below the surfaces! Never search the deep! Make love as if it were a tourney of jests; die as if it were a riddle well guessed! Be scintillantly versatile, rather than thorough; hide your ignorance with bland blasedom; treat tragedy as an intruder, comedy as a chum, and as a reward you will be called ' up-to-date.' Nay, more: your fashionable friends may even mispronounce French in your behalf and dub you *fin de siecle!*"

Dick shuddered laughingly. "A horrible philosophy," he said. And yet he was glad of the other's bitterness; it showed, through all its veil of sneers and scorn, something of the point of view of the foremost in that race toward Death that some of the town·dwellers are wont to call Life.

Yet he could not keep his thoughts long on the serious import of the other's scornful flippancy. How shall two-and-twenty years, and health, and sunshine, and a spirit susceptible to enjoyments that the very atmosphere seemed rendolent of, allow a young man to brood on the progress of the world's cancer? No; there were too many distractions! Tandems whirling by with horsy young men handling the ribbons; brakes full of laughing girls and straw-hatted young men; hackney carriages with four occupants unmistakably of the bookmaker guild.

Just before they rolled into sight of the grand-stand, Stanley said, "Oh, who do you suppose I had a letter from yesterday?"

" No idea."

"The most noble A. B. Wooton, of the late lamented *Torch*."

" You don't say so. His nerve never dies, eh?"

" As I said before, his is not a case of 'nerve'; it is genius. He has the prettiest story you ever read, swears his advertising man deceived him and got the paper into all manner of tight places; found himself forced to get away from the ruins so that he could the better repay his creditors, which he states he has instructed his lawyers to do, and all the rest of it! I don't believe a word of it; but he has got grit!"

"That is a national fault," said Dick soberly, "the admiration of 'grit' in scoundrels. For that is all that Wooton is, after all!"

"Oh, well, why split hairs? He never did you any harm, did he? However, about his letter. He writes from Dresden. Says he has just met some Americans—name of Ware, I think. Enjoying himself immensely—girl in the party —moonlight rides and all that sort of thing. Wonder how long he'll last over there?"

"I know some Wares," said Dick quietly; "but I hardly think it could be the same ones. Though they are in Europe just now, that's true." His thoughts tried to hark back to Lincolnville, to his parting with Dorothy Ware, and to her return; but the present was too strong for him. They were driving across the course at this moment, and over into the field, which was already a motly, colored mass of vehicles, white dresses, parasols and stamping horses. The tops of coaches were made over into sitting room for summer-dressed girls, of whose faces one caught only the white under-half—the chin and the mouth, in high sun relief—while the eyes were in shade of the huge parasols. One caught glimpses of light shoes and hose; of young men walking, in earnest converse over betting tickets held in hand; of wicker lunch-baskets being brought from the inner chambers of the coaches and 'prepared for a future hunger; and, beyond, in the grand stand, of a black, indistinguishable mass of spectators, noisy, tremendous.

As soon as they had found a place for the dog-cart, from which they would be able to see the finish with tolerable comfort and completeness, Stanley said, with a noticeable alacrity succeeding the languid pessimism that had distinguished him all during the drive down.

"Now then, Lancaster, let's hurry over to the betting-shed!"

For a moment only Dick hesitated. "Going to bet, or just to look on?" he asked.

"Bet, of course, you innocent infant! But, Scotland, you don't have to! You can just soak in the—what do you call it—the inpressionistic view of it. But hurry up, whatever you are going to do, I don't want the odds to tumble down too far before I get there!"

Not so long ago Dick would have cavilled, hesitated, perhaps refused. Now he caught his half-uttered objections being met by a whisper in his own mind of 'Don't be a prig!' and he followed Stanley silently. It occurred to him, presently, that to warn oneself of becoming a prig was in itself evidence of priggishness. Impatiently he shook his head, as if to get all analytical reflections out of his head altogether. He looked at the scene around him, and forgot everything else.

The scene in the betting-shed was, just as is the stock exchange floor, the boiling-point of the kettle of froth called metropolitan life. Around the book-makers' stands was a seething, struggling mass of humanity. Each member of this mob was pushing, striving, perspiring for —what?—the chance to get something for nothing! The bookmakers them-selves were straining every nerve to keep pace with the public's feverish desire to get rid of it's money. On their little stands, their heads on a level with the black-board that furnished the names of the horses and the odds against, they stood; one hand busy taking in money that was handed in to the inner part of the stand, the other grasping the piece of chalk that ever and again touched the black-board to effect some change in the odds. One man inside was busy with pencil and paper, registering each ticket as it was handed out; another covered the face of the ticket with the hasty hieroglyphics that stood for the horse chosen and the amount wagered and the amount that might be won. Here and there a bookmaker encouraged the "plunge" on some horse that he professed to scorn by shouting forth his odds and the horse's name. The blind struggle of the majority was an amusing spectacle; it certainly seemed to vouch for the truth of the saying that man is a gambling animal. Like serpents, the "touts," professional vendors of spurious stable information, went winding in and out through the throng, sometimes dis-playing judgment in the would-be bettors they approached, but as often as not displaying most lamentable indiscretion.

Dick watched, with an amused smile, how one of these fellows sided up to a quiet man, who, program in hand, was leaning against a pillar watching the boards and the changes in odds. The quiet man listened to the tout's hoarse whisperings, and then threw his coat back showing an "owner's" badge. The tout slunk sheepishly into the crowd.

"If you take my advice," said Stanley who was fighting his way towards some remote goal or other, "you'll take a little flyer on Dr. Rice. That's what I'm going to do. There's a fellow on the other side of the ring has him a point higher than anyone else."

Dick, without having made up his mind as to his own betting or not betting, helped his companion in his struggle to get through the crowd. Desperate energy was necessary. There was never any time for apologies; elbows were pushed into sides, toes were trodden on, scarfs twisted and sleeve-links broken; no matter, there was money to be won and there was no time either to consider passing annoyances or the posibility of loss.

"Ah," said Stanley, finally, as they found themselves in front of a blackboard that had a figure "7" chalked to the left of the name Dr. Rice and a "3" to the right. "Here we are! Now then, what are you going to do?" He whipped out a twenty dollar bill and crumpled it carefully into the palm of his hand.

Dick thought quickly. After all, it was merely the foregoing of some luxury or another; he would postpone joining that polo club, perhaps, or go without that new edition of Menzel's drawing's that he had been promising himself. He took a bill out of his card-case and handed it, without a word, to Stanley.

The ticket that Stanley presently handed him had "Rice" almost illigibly scrawled across it, and the figures "70" and " 10." Dick stood to lose ten or to win seventy dollars.

By the time they had got comfortably ensconsed in their seats in the dog-cart once more, the horses were at the post for the great event of the day, the American Derby. Dick had begun to feel something of the torment of expectation and fear and hope that makes the gambler's nerves either like a sheet of reeds in the wind or like a tightly-drawn wire. If he won it would be, as he heard some men in the betting-shed remark, "just like finding money." He could allow himself all sorts of extravagances. He observed the horses making false start after false start without even a suspicion of qualmishness as to the moral aspect of the case coming over him. He had grown, to use his own phase, broader.

Down beyond the turn into the stretch was the bunch of restless horses, the vari-colored jackets, the starter's carriage, and the assistant starter's flag. There was the sky-blue jacket that showed where the favorite, The Ghost, was pirouetting on his hind legs; the black and yellow bars of Ætna's jockey, and many others. But Dick's eyes were focused on Dr. Rice; the horse's jockey was in all-black.

"Ah—h!" The vast crowd roars and cheers as a start is made. All together, like a herd of cattle, they sweep on toward the grand-stand. It is not racing yet. Favorite and second favorite are back in the centre of the bunch. In front of the grand-stand one jockey sends his horse out a length in front. It is an outsider, but there are plenty of backers of outsiders, and a cheer goes up. "He'll walk away from them!" "The others are standing still!" and such-like shouts go up. The pace begins to get killing. At the half Ætna is seen to move up to the leader, finally to pass him. The favorite is also creeping from out the ruck. Slowly, surely he forges past all the leaders but Ætna; the latter shoots ahead again for the distance of a length and The Ghost drops back to fourth place. It was evidently merely a feeler to find out whether Ætna was going too fast or whether there was still time to get up when the stretch was reached.

Round the turn they sweep into the stretch. It is a dangerous picture, with so many horses so close together, with such speed, and such possibility of collisions. But the turn is made in a second; now they are in the straight road for home. The Ghost is creeping up again, wearing down horse after horse, finally reaching Ætna's throatlatch. Neck and neck these two race up the last furlong; then a sudden, surprised roar breaks out from the mob of onlookers; another horse has cut loose from the bunch that has now become a straggling, attenuated string of tired horses. The shout goes up: "Look at Dr. Rice!" "Dr. Rice!"

Now he is up to Ætna's flanks and going under a pull; his jockey has never yet touched spur to him. The whip comes down on Ætna; it is no use; he is raced out. Now Dr. Rice has reached The Ghost, and the latter's jockey begins using the whip. In the grand-stand there is an inferno of cheering; men are shouting themselves hoarse, and jumping up and down in nervous paroxysms. Dr. Rice's jockey never moves a muscle to all appearances. The cries go up from the mob: "Come Rice!" "Come Ghost!" The judges begin to strain their their attention to the viewing of a very close finish. Then with a final mighty lift, Dr. Rice, in the very last stride, shoots forward under the wire a neck in front of The Ghost.

Dr. Rice has won.

On the way home Stanley was another man. He talked as if such a thing as a regret for a lost youth had never entered his head; he was young again. He recounted his impression of the race, asked Dick what he had thought of it all, was full of amusing anecdotes about men who had tried to get him to back the favorite, and was fertile in suggestions for what they should do that evening. Of course it was understood they must celebrate in some way. Surely! Surely!

"Oh," he said, finally, "I know what we'll do. We'll go along to the Imperial Theatre. I know some of the girls in the burlesque there. I'll introduce you. We'll enjoy ourselves."

Dick began to demur.

"Don't be a d——d idiot," said the other man, half smiling, half frowning.

CHAPTER VII

NO one that has ever been in Dresden is likely to forget the beauties of the Bruehlsche Terrasse. The cool plash of waters from the Elbe come up invitingly; the green of the neighboring gardens is luscious, and there are nearly always strains of music in the air. Especially pleasing is the picture on a summer's evening.

In one of the concert gardens they give out on the Terrasse, there sat at a small round table, one dreemy midsummer evening, Mrs. Ware and her daughter, Dorothy. In front of them were small cups of coffee, and such appetising rolls as only the Conditors of the continent can make. The garden was in no wise different from a thousand others to be found in German cities; save only that it was especially happy in its location. There was a light, gravelly soil; a multitude of round tables; chairs occupied by a cosmopolitan crew of both sexes; at one end, in the shadow of huge lime trees, was the *Capelle*. Over all was the star-gemmed sky. The air was sweet with the song of the violins, and the cheery laughter of the many family parties came echoing along from time to time in musical accompaniment. There were German students, with the

vari-colored caps and occasional sword-
wounds on their faces; officers with
clanking swords and clothes fitting in
lines that suggested stays; English
tourists, easily distinguishable by costumes they would not have dared to startle
Hyde Park with; Americans with high
pitched voices; and a few Russians, ex-
cessively polite of manner and cruel of
eye.

Miss Dorothy Ware was engaged in
munching at a roll that had been steep-
ing in the strong coffee, when she suddenly turned to her mother with an
eager exclamation.

"I declare, mamma," she said, "if
there isn't Mr. Wooton coming this
way. The idea of meeting him again at
all. I'm sure I never thought we would;
there are so many people away traveling about this time of the year, and there
are so many places. He has just seen us,
mamma, and he's coming over here. See
he's lifting his hat. I'm glad we've got
this vacant chair."

Wooton shook hands with them. "The
old platitude about the world being a
very small place seems to strike true,"
he said. "Do you know, it's a positive
relief to talk to people of my own sort
once more." He had sat down beside
Dorothy, and placed his stick and gloves
on the gravel beside him. He looked
decidedly handsome; his small mouth
seemed smaller than ever, and his face
was paler than when he dictated the
fortunes of the *Torch*. He was scrupu-
lously dressed; every detail was so nicely adjusted that he would have success-

fully run the gauntlet of all the comment of Piccadilly and Broadway.

"I've just come from Berlin," he went on, "it was like an oven there. Nearly everybody was away; some of them in Heringsdorf, some in Switzerland, some down in this district. My compartment in the train was filled with a lot of officers on leave, and they talked army slang until my head swam, and I would have given gold for the sound of an American voice."

"You seem to rush about a good deal," ventured Mrs. Ware. "Din't we meet you in Schwalbach?"

"Mamma forgets so," put in Dorothy, "she's been meeting so many people, I begin to think she jumbles them all up. But it was in Schwalbach, mamma; you're right. Don't you remember? We were sitting near the Stahlbrunnen, with the Tremonts — we used to set next to them at the Hotel d'Europe— when Mr. Wooton came up and said how-d'ye-do to the Tremonts, and they presented him to us. When Mrs. Tremont was at boarding-school, you know," she went on, turning to Wooton, "she and mamma were great chums. She was a Miss Alexander." She put her hand up to her hat and gave it a mysterious pressure, presumably to rectify some invisable displacement. She turned and looked out into the darkness whence came the sullen swish of the river. "It was delightful in Schwalbach," she said finally.

"It was horribly expensive," commented Mrs. Ware, sipping her coffee.

"But the waters did you good, I hope?" inquired Wooton, suavely solicitous.

"Oh, I guess so. But I don't seem to improve right along, as I should? But I shouldn't complain. I'm a good deal stouter than when I left home. Besides, Dorothy is having a right good time."

"Ah," smiled Wooton, to the girl, "you like it—the life here?"

"Yes; I like it. I don't say that I like it better than other things. But who could help liking that?" She swept her parasol around so that it pointed out toward the river. There was complete darkness there, lit up occasionally by the lights of passing steamers. Fog-whistles sounded occasionally; on the opposite shore there was a dim glow of yellow lights. The water sobbed ceaselessly; there was a mist rising, and the steamer lights began to seem hazier than ever, mere golden circles hanging in the dense darkness. The violins were playing something of Waldteufel's.

It was true; not even the most patriotic of Americans .could have helped granting that all this was very pleasant. Dorothy Ware had certainly given up being half-hearted in her enthusiasm for European things; they had met so many people and had rubbed up against so much of cosmopolitanism that unconsciously she had come to see that to apply the narrow Lincolnville view to all the people she saw now was a trifle absurd. She gave herself candidly over to enjoy it all. That was what she had come for. And it must be confessed that, during this process of enjoyment, her memories of her former self became ghosts of ever-increasing vagueness. When she caught herself thinking of Dick Lancaster it was usually to wonder what sort of a girl he had married. She smiled when she thought of the things he had said to her before they parted. It didn't seem to touch her at all now, and she seemed sure that a man slips out of that sort of thing much earlier than the woman.

They met Wooton a good deal after that. He spent a good deal of time among the pictures, and when they visited the *Gruene Gwoeble* they found him there. He was invariably bright and amusing; he offered to pilot them and smooth things for them generally; Mrs. Ware began to think he was tremendously nice. She remembered that Miss Alexander—now Mrs. Tremont—had always been one of the most aristocratic of girls; she recalled with something of a shudder, her own awe at her school-mate's lengthy dissertation upon blood and family and kindred subjects. So, she argued, if Wooton was in Mrs. Tremont's set in town, there was certainly not the vestige of a doubt concerning his being eminently the correct thing. She had lived in the country so long herself that she admitted she was no longer able to note the difference between good coin and bad; but she had infinite faith in Mrs. Tremont. Dorothy, too, got to feel that he was very charming; he was so handsome, and dressed so well. It was very pleasant to have him in the party; he added distinction.

Wooton had admitted that he knew young Lancaster; he divined that she had liked the boy; he was wise enough to tell her only pleasant things about Dick. The only thing Dorothy objected to was that Wooton went about a good deal with the Tremonts. It seemed to her that he was quite devoted to Miss Eugenie.

" I don't like her a bit," she told him rather tactlessly, speaking of Miss Tremont, " she's so supercilious. I never know when she's laughing at me and when she's not listening to me. I suppose she thinks I'm a country chit and don't know anything. But I wouldn't be clever the way she's clever for anything in the world. Why does she have to sneer at innocence and goodness? Nobody ever accused her of either, did they?"

Which, Wooton thought to himself, was not half bad. As a matter of fact he enjoyed being with Eugene Tremont immensely. She was one of those intensely modern girls that the world is so unhappily rich in just now. She would talk about any subject under the sun. She declared that she had always cared more for male society anyway; she despised her own sex and said spiteful things about it. She pretended to be completely cognizant of all the wickedness there was in the world; and she went on the presumption that man was a sort of infernal machine that there was unlimited fun—the fun of danger—in handling. Men liked her at first invariably; there was something refreshing and stimulating in the nonchalance with which she ·tabooed no subject from her conversa.ion ; they said to themselves that this was a person, thank goodness, whom one did not eternally have to consider in the light of a sex, but rather of a sexless cleverness. But, somehow or other, her cleverness wearied presently; she palled as all surfaces must inevitably pall. Wooton, however, turned to her because she was of his own special calibre— all cleverness, and no apparent sharply defined system of conduct. With the Wares he was so perpetually on a gridiron; he was afraid of saying something that would startle them. They amused him, these people, with their simplicity, their taking virtue for granted and vice for an abhorent mystery! To talk to them it was necessary to keep a constant check on his cynical; while with Eugene Tremont it was sword to sword, a sharp continuous fencing with verbal weapons.

So, when Dorothy Ware made the cutting little speech about Miss Tremont, Wooton told himself that there was something more than mere dislike for the Boston . girl at the bottom of it. Considering the matter, he broke into a laugh. Was it possible, h'm. That would really be too rich.

He began to be seen with the Tremonts oftener than ever. He went with them to the opera, he took a seat in their landau. He went to Teplitz with them.

"They're more in the same set, I suppose," said Mrs. Ware, when Dorothy spoke of it. "He was at college with her brother, too; I guess they talk about him a good deal."

Dorothy guessed that she knew better; but she said nothing. Somehow, Dresden began to seem fearfully dreary. She began importuning her mother to pack up and go to Munich; they had some friends there. Dorothy declared Dresden made her homesick; she said it was all so small and pretty, anyway; it wasn't a metropolis, yet it tried to ape the real article. And then there were so many Americans—you couldn't talk English anywhere without having people understand you, which was distinctly annoying, because occasionally one likes to make personal asides about costumes and hats and complexions—and, well, what was the use of staying there any longer anyhow? But Mrs. Ware declared the climate agreed with her. She said she hadn't felt so well for ever so long, she wasn't going to try any other place as this one agreed with her. Did Dorothy want to see her die? No; Dorothy did not. She submitted, and went about looking dismal.

And then, one day, the sunshine came back into here face once more. It was not that the good fairies had remodeled the town of Dresden; it was not that all English-speaking people had suddenly deserted the place; in fact, it was hard to say just what made the difference. It was just possible that Wooton's return from Teplitz had something to do with the good humor in which Dorothy came back to her mother that noon, after a walk down to the Conditorei. She had almost cannoned into him, rounding a corner; they had shaken hands; he had avowed the pleasure he felt at seeing her again. It is just possible that the sight of this young man was a talisman for Miss Ware's temper; it is at least certain that her melancholia was gone.

He called on them, in a day or so, at their apartments in the Hotel Bellevue. Mrs. Ware was very glad to see him; she was more vivacious than she had yet shown herself. She proposed that they take their coffee out in the garden, on the river front, under the trees. They sat watching the boats, and the little boys paddling about barefooted; it was in the cool of sunset, and there were red bars slanting across the western horizon. It was very pleasant. The waiter moved about noiselessly; there were some children making merry in the swing set up at the far end of the garden.

"Is Teplitz very full?" asked Mrs. Ware.

"Yes; more people than usual, I believe. I should think the hot baths would do you good, too, Mrs. Ware?"

"Oh, I guess I'll stay here a while yet. I'm getting to feel quite spry again. You left the Tremonts there?"

"Yes?"

Dorothy turned away from the river and looked at him a trifle reproachfully. "You must be awfully fond of those people," she said, trying to smile.

Wooton shrugged his shoulders carelessly.

"No," he replied, "I can't say that exactly. But Mrs. Tremont really insisted on my going; she said she had never been there before, and thought that as I knew the ropes of the place, it would be a small thing for me to play pilot for them for a while. What was I to do?" He looked at Dorothy appealingly.

Mrs. Ware was pushing a stray wisp of hair from her cheek.

"In Boston, Dorothy," she said, "I guess Mrs. Tremont is quite a society leader." She said it as if that was an assertion of crushing significance, intended to quiet any possible questionings as to why any young man should think it necessary to comply with the wishes of so great a personage.

"What if she is?" was Dorothy's quick reply; "that doesn't make her any better, does it? I don't see how you can go around with them so much, that's all, Mr. Wooton."

"Oh," he laughed, "I assure you I don't like them so very much myself; but I don't dislike them. And I hate to offend people. They asked me to go!"

They drank their coffee, and watched the twilight settling down. They talked lightly, and laughed a good deal.

Miss Ware," Wooton asked presently, "you've never been down to Schandau, have you?"

"No. Is it worth while?"

"Immensely! You ought to make the trip."

"Oh, I simply can't begin to get mamma

to move from this town. She's perfectly enchanted with it, somehow." She
looked at her mother, and patted her on
the arm. Mrs. Ware said nothing, only
smiled back at her daughter, who went
on, "but I'd like it mightily."

"I wish you'd let me show you the
place," Wooton persevered. He looked
over at Mrs. Ware in a hesitating way.
"Perhaps—if Mrs. Ware would rather
not stir from the hotel—there would be
no objection to Miss Ware making the
trip with me? The place is really pretty;
the royal residence there is one of the
sights. It's only half an hour or so by
the steamer. You'd hardly notice our
absence; I think she'd enjoy it." He
wondered a little whether they would
look at him in frigid horror, or take it as
a proposition quite in accord with the
conventions they were accustomed to.
He knew perfectly well that most of the
people he knew in the East would have
considered him insane if he had ventured such a proposal; but, in regard to
these people, and this girl in particular,
he remembered that a friend of his had
once used a phrase that had struck him
at the time as rather good, and that was,
perhaps, applicable. The man had
declared, half in a spirit of banter, half
in chivalrous defense, that the girl of
the West paraphrased the old motto to
read: "*Sans peur, sans reproche et sans
chaperon.*"

To his relief, Mrs. Ware's answer was
merely a smile at her daughter, and a
"You'll have to see what Dorothy thinks
about it, I guess. It's her picnic. If she

wares to go—." She left the sentence unfinished, as if to convey the impression that under the circumstances mentioned her own preference would be allowed lapse.

"I think," said Dorothy, with a little clasping together of her hands, "that it would be simply delightful! You wouldn't worry, would you, mamma? There are always so many waiters around and—dear, dear, I talk just as if we were going this very minute!" She looked gratefully at Wooton. Somehow or other, he felt himself blushing. He caught himself regretting the fact that he was no longer as genuine as this girl was. "I think it's simply perfect of you to ask me," she went on, "I'm sure I'll enjoy it ever so much."

"Then," he said, airily, "we'll consider that settled. It's very good of you to say you'll go, I'm sure. Suppose we say Wednesday?"

CHAPTER VIII

IT was certainly a sunny enough day, and the Elbe glistened invitingly. Wooton had been up earlier than was usual for him and had taken a walk out into the level country; when he came into the hallway of the Bellevue he was in the best of spirits. Miss Ware came down the stairway, presently, her parasol in rest over her left arm, and her gloves still in process of being buttoned. She smiled down at him radiantly.

"I haven't kept you waiting, have I?"
she cried.

"Not a moment," he answered," adding, with a smile, "strange to say.
You young ladies usually do! But—do
you notice how kind the clerk of the
weather is?"

"Delightful!" They went slowly down
toward the wharf where the little steamer
was puffing lazily in the rising heat.

"Your mother is well?" He asked the
question as solicitously as if he were the
family physician.

"Quite well. The fact is," she added
with a comic effort to seem melancholy,
"I'm afraid she'll be so well soon that
she'll want to go back to the States.

"Ah, so you don't want to go just
yet?"

"Oh, I haven't half seen it all, you
know! Still,—" she sighed gently and
looked out beyond the real horizon, "it
will be nice to be home again."

Wooton brought a couple of steamer
chairs and placed them on the deck-space
that was well in the shadow of the awning. The sun was beginning to grow
almost unpleasantly strong. Presently,
with a minute or so of wriggling away
from the wharf, of backing and sidling,
the little steamer got proper headway
and proceeded slowly on its way up the
river. The central portion of the town
was soon passed; green garden-spaces,
and houses shut in by cherry-trees, gave
way to low-lying meadows and hills rising
up in the distance. The perpetual "shug-
shug-shug" of the engines, and the
hushed whispering of the river as the

steamer bows cut through the water were almost the only sounds that broke the quiet. There was not a cloud in the sky. Swallows darted arrow-like through the air.

Wooton had pushed his hat back from his forehead and sat with half-closed eyes. He was silent. Miss Ware, looking at him shyly, wondered what he was thinking about; told herself once more that he was the handsomest man she had ever seen, and then sent her clear gaze riverward again. What Wooton was thinking at that moment was that he would give many things if in his spirit there were still that simplicity that would ask of life no more feverish pleasures than those he was now enjoying—the pleasures of peace and quiet. To be able to sit thus, with half-closed eyes, as it were, and let the wind of the world always blow merely a gentle breath across one's face!—perhaps, after all, that was the road to happiness. On the other hand, the thousand and one experiences missed, the opportunities wasted! Surely it was impossible to appreciate the sweets of good had one not first tasted of the fruit of knowledge of evil! But supposing one so got the taste of the bitter apple into one's mouth that thereafter all things tasted bitter and the good, especially, created only nausea? For that was his own state. Well, in that case—he smiled to himself in his silence—there was nothing to be done but enjoy, enjoy to think of the once easily reached contentment as of a dream that is dead, and to strive so ceaselessly to blow the embers of the fires of pleasure that they would at least keep smouldering until all the vessel was ashes. The pleasures of the moment—those were the things to seize! The moment was the thing to enjoy; the morrow might not come.

He turned to look at the girl beside him, who had by this time resigned herself with something of quiet amusement to his silence, and now sat, veilless, her lips slightly open to the breeze, her face unspeakably fair-seeming with its rosy flush and its look of eager, expectant enjoyment. He told himself that, as far as this moment at least went, it left little to be desired; to sit beside so sweet a girl as Dorothy Ware was surely pleasure enough. And then he thought somewhat grimly that he himself was, unfortunately, impregnable to the infection of such simple joys.

"A penny!" he spoke softly, as if not to wake her too brusquely from a reverie.

"Oh," she cried, with a little start, and turning toward him, "they are not worth so much, really! I was thinking of Mr. Lancaster. He used to be so terribly ambitious; you know. Didn't you say you knew of him, in town?"

Wooton realized that he must needs be diplomatic. He called it diplomacy; some persons might have rudely termed it mendacity. The two are commonly confounded.

"Yes," he replied, "some artists that I knew used to mention his name occasionally." He paused an instant or two and then continued, impassively, "I seem to remember hearing someone say that he was engaged to some very rich girl."

Dorothy Ware smiled sadly. "I supposed he would be," she said, simply. She felt angry at herself for not feeling the news more deeply; yet it hardly seemed to touch her at all; it was just as if she had heard that one of her girl friends had married. She recalled Dick's impassioned, if soberly worded, farewell; she remembered her own words; she wondered how it was possible that the passing months could have changed her so that now she seemed almost indifferent as to young Lancaster's fortunes or misfortunes.

Wooton's exclamation of "Ah, there's Schandau!" broke in upon the train of her self-questioning thoughts. They walked over to the rail of the boat together, and looked out to where the roofs of summer-villas and hotels came peeping through the wooded banks of the river. As they stood thus she felt his right hand just touching her own left. Somehow, the blood came rushing into her face, and she took her hand away under pretense of fastening up her veil.

From the landing-stage they walked up to one of the hotels, where Wooton ordered a light repast. Miss Ware was in excellent spirits. The beauty of the day and the picturesqueness of the place, with its cozy villas tucked away against the hillside, its leafy lanes and its mountain shadows, filled her with the elixir of happiness. She chatted and laughed incessantly. She asked Wooton if they couldn't go for a walk into the woods. Walk, of course! No, she didn't want to drive; that was too much like poking along the boulevards at home in the States. She wanted to stroll up little foot-paths, into the heart of the wood, and gather flowers, and have the birds whistle to her! Didn't he remember that she was a country girl? She hadn't been in a real wood since she left Lincolnville, and did he suppose she was going to enjoy this one by halves?

They walked out along the white, dusty *chaussee* until it reached the denser part of the hill-forest; then they struck off into a by-path. In the shadow of the pines it was cool and refreshing; the scent of pines filled the air. In the thick under-growth there were occasional clumps of blue-berries. Dorothy Ware picked them eagerly, laughing carelessly when she stained her gloves with the juice. She plucked flowers in abundance, and had Wooton carry them. They strayed heedlessly into the forest, hardly noting whether they followed the path or not. They found themselves, presently, in the lee of a huge rock that some long-silent volcanic upheaval must once have thrust through the earth's shell. Close to the earth this rock was narrower than at its summit; under its sloping base there was a cavity all covered with moss. Over-head the pines shut out the sky.

A trifle tired with her walk, Miss Ware hailed the sight of this spot with unfeigned gladness. Wooton spread his top-coat for her. Sitting there, in the silence made voiceful by the rustling of the pines, Wooton felt his heart beat faster than it had in years. She was pretty, this girl; her voice was so caressing, and her presence and manner such a charm! Young enough, too, to be taught many things. He watched her, as she sat there, binding the flowers with the stems of long grasses, stray curls playing about her cheeks, and her mouth showing the slight down on the upper lip, and, for an instant, there came to him a feeling of pity. It is possible, perhaps, that the serpent occasionally pauses to admire the pigeon's plumage.

"I wonder," he began, softly, "whether you know Hugh McCulloch's 'Scent o' Pines'? No? I think you will like it:

Love shall I liken thee unto the rose
   That is so sweet ?
Nay, since for a single day she grows,
   Then scattered lies upon the garden-rows
   Beneath our feet.

But to the perfume shed when forests nod,
   When noonday shines;
That lulls us as we tread the wood-land sod,
   Eternal as the eternal peace of God—
   The scent o' pines.

He quoted the verses musically. He gave the words all the sincerity that never found its way into his actions. He was one of those men who read a thing better than the man that wrote it, because they know better the art of simulating an emotion that he knows only how to feel.

" A pretty idea," she admitted. They talked on ramblingly, lightly. Overhead the sun was sinking into the west. A wind had sprung up from the south-west, and in the north-west banks of clouds had gathered, thick and threatening. Occasional flashes of lightning darted across the cloud-space. A thunderstorm was evidently approaching, proceeding stubbornly against the wind. The sun dipped behind the clouds, that rose higher, presently over-casting all the heavens. Light gusts of wind went puffing through the forest, scattering leaves and whirling twigs.

Suddenly, with a crash and a roar, the mountain storm broke over the forest. Almost on the stroke of the first flash of lightning came the thunder; then as if the clouds had been bulls charging in the arena, the furious concussion was followed by the gush of the blood of heaven. The rain came down in lances that struck the earth and bounded up again. About the heads of the pines the wind roared and wailed.

Coming upon them so suddenly, this riot of the elements made the two young people sitting there in the lee of the rock, start to their feet in dismay. A momentary gleam came into Wooton's eyes; whether it was anger or joy only himself could have told. All about them the storm was playing its tremendous tarantelle; the whole earth seemed to shake with the repeated cannonades of the thunderous artillery of the heavens, and through the darkness that had fallen the lightning sent such vivid streaks of light as only made the succeeding gloom more dismal. It was to tempt fate to venture out of the shelter the rock was giving. Instinctively the girl shrank a little toward Wooton. She looked at him appealingly. "It's dreadful," she said, "it—it hurts my eyes so! And—the steamer! Mamma will think—" She stopped and covered her eyes with her hands just as another flash seared its way into the forest.

Wooton stood still, biting his under-lip nervously. "I—I'm afraid it's all my fault," he said, "I ought to have known it was getting late. And these storms come up so quickly here in the mountains. We can't stir from here. The storm is playing right around this wood. It means waiting." He saw her shivering slightly. Bending down, he picked up his top-coat, and put it gently about her shoulders. "You'll catch cold," he warned, in a tender voice.

She said nothing; but he could see gratitude in her eyes. Something seemed to draw her toward him. At each glaring flash she shrank nearer to him. He was looking tensely at her, his hand against a ledge of rock, lest the gusts of wind should swing him out into the open.

A crash that seemed to deafen all hearing for several instants; a flying mass of splintered wood, torn from a suddenly stricken tree that fell straight across the opening of their shelter; a light so white that it hurt the eyes; and a trembling under foot that shook the very ground these two storm-stayed ones stood. In the instant that followed the crash Wooton felt the girl beside him lean heavily towards him; her eyes were closed; she had fainted. Keeping her tightly in his arms, a queer smile played about the corners of his mouth. "It was ordained!" His thoughts uttered themselves almost unconsciously. Holding her so, with the thunder still rolling its chariot wheels all about the reverberate rocks, he kissed her.

The wind veered about, sending the rain spatteringly into their faces. Wooton unfastened the girl's veil, and took her hat off, very gently and carefully. The rain splashed into her face, streaming over the brow and the heavy lashes.

Slowly the lashes lifted; her breast moved in a tremulous breath. As comprehension of her position came to her awakening faculties she seemed to shudder a little, to attempt withdrawal; then her eyes sought his, and something found there seemed to soothe; she sighed again and sank more closely into his embrace. And now fires went coursing through the man; he pressed the girl's slight body to him fiercely, and kissing her upon both eyes, whispered into the rosy shell of her ear, "Dorothy—I love you!"

The storm still played relentlessly about them. The rain came further and further into the shelter-hole. But these two, lip to lip, and breath to breath, gave no heed save to the promptings of their own emotions. The elements might rend the rocks; but hearts they could not scar! The girl felt herself irresistibly drawn by this man. Something in him had always attracted her wonderfully—something she had never

sought to explain, scarcely heeding it
for any length of time. But now that
chance had, as it seemed, thrown the magnet and the steel so closely together, she
felt this hidden, mysterious force more
mightily than ever; it seemed to her
that in his kisses all the earth might melt
away and become nothing. Moments
when she feared him, when he inspired
her with something not unlike anger,
were succeeded by moments when she
felt that he had put an arrow into her
heart which to withdraw meant unutter-
able anguish; but which to bury more
deeply meant the bitterest and sweetest
of the bitter-sweets of love.

While the storm raged on and over
the mountain, these two sat there where
whatsoever forest-gods of love there be
had drawn their magic circle. Reeling
over the mountain top like a drunken
man, the storm passed on along the
river-banks, waking up echoes in the
Bastei, and flying, presently, into Austria.
Its muttered curses grew fainter and
fainter, gradually to be swallowed up
altogether in the swaying of the pines
and the streaming of the rain.

Then, presently, the pines began to
lift their heads again, to shake themselves as if in angry impatience, so that
the rain dropped heavily, and after the
flying column of darkness, light came in
once more from the west. The sun was
still above the horizon. Turning the
rain-drops into opals that glistened with
the rain-bow hues, the sunshine streamed
over the forest. The afternoon, that had
seen such a terrible battle of the ele-

ments, was to die in peace, and light, and sweetness.

They walked together to an eminence that was almost bared of trees. Below them the forest swept in every direction like a field of dark grass. The sun sent its last rays ricochetting over the waves of green to where they stood, silently. Another instant, and the great bronzed body was below the line of hills that made the horizon; only the salmon-colored streaks that stained the lower strata of the western sky remained to tell the tale of the sun-god's day. The air grew slightly chill.

With that first forerunner of the fall of night, there came into the dream that Dorothy Ware had moved in, the chilling thought of—certain facts. They had most assuredly missed the boat back to Dresden. Would there be another when they reached Schandau? Could they get home by carriage?

Wooton could only shrug his shoulders in despair. He did not know. He had counted only on the two hours—the hour of the departure from Dresden and the return from Schandau; the storm had upset all his plans. He was utterly at sea; he could say nothing until they reached Schandau and made inquiries. Would she not let the thought drop until then. Was there not the sweet present?

As they walked through the forest, picking their way as best they could, without a compass, and uncertain whether their direction was the right one or the wrong one, night falling surely and swiftly, Wooton held his arm about the young girl's waist, lest she stumble or slip. She looked up at him smilingly and trustingly, yet tremulous at the behest of that mysterious something that drove her to accept his caresses instead of spurning them, that made her quiver at his touch, like a wind-kissed aspen, and had her still the storm within her by giving it a storm to fight.

The darkness became denser. Their feet stumbled, and trees were hardly distinguishable in the blackness. Had there been no other thought save that considering their condition and surroundings, the girl, at least, would have been trembling in fear and and uncertainty. As it was, each loophole for a doubt was closed up by a kiss.

A streak of white came suddenly in view, and they found themselves upon the chaussee once more. But in which direction lay Chandau? Overhead the the stars were shining, but neither of these two could use the night heavens as a chart.

Behind them came the dull rumble of wheels. Around a turn of the road came carriage-lights. As they flashed close upon them, Wooton spoke to the driver.

"Sie fahren nach Schandau?" nicht wahr?

The driver assented, without stopping. At the sound of the questioner's voice, one of the occupants of the carriage had leaned window-ward.

It was Miss Tremont, of Boston. In the glare of the lanterns she had caught the faces plainly.

She leaned back to the cushions, smiling slightly.

CHAPTER IX

IT'S dark as an inferno, and the stairs make a man's back ache," said Laurance Stanley dismally to himself, as he climbed up to the Philistine Club, "but," as he caught his breath again and consequently began to feel more cheerful, "it's comfortable when you get there.

Which was distinctly true. The furniture, the carpets, the hangings in the spacious, rambling old rooms were all ancient and worn, but comfort was as common to them all as was age. When you came in and slid down into the shiny leather cavern of an arm chair you felt that you were at home. At least, the men who were members did. They were a queer lot, these members. Just what they had in common, no man might say; there were artists, and writers, and musicians, and men-about-town. To outsiders it seemed as if a certain sort of cleverness was the open sesame to the membership rolls. In the matter of name, it was doubtless, the effect of a stroke of humor that came to one of the founders. Perhaps, for the very reason that most of the members were men of the sort that one instinctively knew to be modern, and broad and untramelled by dogmas or doctrines, the club had been named the Philistine Club. It was no longer in its first youth. The walls were behung with the portraits of former presidents—portraits that were all alike in their effect of displaying an execrable sort of painting; it was evident that in its selection of painters in ordinary the club had lived strictly up to its name. The building that housed the club was an old one, on one of the busiest business thoroughfares in the city. It was very convenient, as the hard-working fellows among the members phrased it; in a minute you could drop out of the rush and roar of the street-traffic into the quiet gloom of the club, a lounge, and a book.

Stanley had not been in the dark corner that he usually affected very long before Vanstruther came in, his beard more pointed than ever. He dropped limply into a chair, put his feet on one of the whist tables, and said, as he lit a cigar: "Do you know this is about the time of year that I realize that this town is a hole? I repeat it—a hole! A hole, moreover, with the bottom out. I tell you there's not a soul in town just now."

"Most true," assented Stanley, "for neither you nor I have anything that deserves the name."

"Bosh! What I mean is that the place is a howling desert. Everybody is still at the seashore, or the mountains, or the mineral springs. Newport or the White Mountains, or Manitou, or Mackinac Island—there's where every self-respecting person is at this time; not in this old sweat-box. Why, it's a positive fact that there are no pretty girls at all on the avenue these days; or, if there are any, you can tell at a glance that they're from Podunk or Egypt."

"In other words, there is a scarcity of 'Mrs. Tomnoddy received yesterday,' and 'there will be a meeting of the Contributors' Club at Mrs. Mausoleum's on Friday.' People who like to see their names in the daily papers are out of town, so the society journalist waileth; is it not so? It all comes down to bread and butter in this country. Just as soon as we get away from bread and butter, we'll be greater idiots than the others ever knew how to be." He waved a hand carelessly to some remote space in which he inferred the continent of Europe.

"That's all very well," rejoined the other, "you are always great on magniloquent generalizations, but you never trouble about the concrete things. I'm up a tree for copy, day in, day out, and I groan just once, and what do you do? You moralize loftily. But do you help me with a real bit of news? Not a bit of it."

"Well, you know," Stanley said, lazily, "I'm the last man in the world to come to for items of news concerning *le monde ou l'm s'amuse*. But if you want something a notch or two lower—say about the grade of members of this club. Do you notice that Dante Belden's sofa is empty today?"

The journalist looked around to the other side of the room where an old black leather lounge stood. It was the sofa that had long since become the special property, in the eyes of the other members, of the artist, Dante Gabriel Belden. He used to sleep there a great deal; and he used to dream also. Occasionally he waxed talkative, and then there usually grew up around him a circle of chairs. In such conclave, there passed anecdotes that were delightful, criticisms that were incisive, and, in total, nothing that was altogether stupid.

"Where is he?" asked Vanstruther.

"Where is who?" It was Marsboro, the *Chronicle's* artist, that had sauntered over.

"Belden."

"Married," said Stanley, laconically.

"The devil!" exclaimed Vanstruther, putting his cigar down on the window-ledge.

"Not the same," was the quiet reply. "Although—" and Stanley paused to smile—"it might be interesting to trace the relationship."

"Oh, talk straight talk for a minute, can't you! I never knew the man was thinking of it."

"Nor did I. Well, we're all friends of his, and men don't think any less of each other in a case of this kind, so I'll tell you the story. In my opinion, it's a clear case of 'Tomlinson, of Berkley Square'. However, that's open to individual interpretation. Belden has succumbed to a lifelong passion for Henri Murger?"

Marsboro swore audibly. "I don't see," he said, that you're any plainer than you were! What's all that got to do with the man's marriage?"

"Everything! Everything—the way I look at it, at least. You know as well as I do, how saturated he is with admiration for those delightful escapades of the Quartier Latin that Muger makes such pretty stories of. Well—he has acted up to them. The trouble is that this is not the Quartier Latin, and that sort of thing is a trifle awkward when you make a Christian ceremony of it. Here are the facts: Belden and myself were coming home from the theatre a good while ago, when we came to a couple that were decidedly in liquor. The man had been out to dinner, or a dance or somewhere; he had his dress clothes on, and his white shirt was still immaculate. His silk hat was on straight enough. His walk was the only thing that betrayed him. He had his arm around the girl. When we passed them, or began to, we could hear that the girl was crying. Her boots were shabby and the skirt that trailed over them was badly fringed at the bottom; above the waist she had on such sham finery and her face, once pretty, had such a stale, hunted look, as told plainly to what class she belonged. The class that is no class at all, and yet that has always been. "I'm afraid of you—you've been drinking—let me go," she was crying out. Belden stopped at once. The man put his arm more tightly about her waist, and tried, drunkenly, to kiss her. The girl wrenched herself almost away from him. She screamed out, "Let loose of me, you beast!" Then she began to moan a little. That settled Bel-

den. He walked in front of the man in
the white shirt-front, and told him to
let the woman go. The man said he
would see him damned first. The words
had hardly tortured their stuttering way
from the drunken man's mouth, before
Belden gave him a blow between the
eyes that sent the fellow to the sidewalk. He lay there cursing, drunkenly.
Belden asked the woman, quietly, where
she lived. She looked at him and
laughed. Laughed aloud! I've seen
most things, in my time, but that
woman's laugh, and the look on her face
are about the most grewsome things I
remember. She laughed, you know as
if someone had just told her that he
would like to walk down to hell with her.
She laughed in that high, unnatural key,
in which only women of that sort can
laugh; it was a laugh that had in it the
scorn of the Devil for his toy, man. There
was in it a memory of a time when she
might have unblushingly answered that
question of 'Where do you live?' There
was in it something like pity for this innocent who asked her that question in
good faith, or seemed to. Then she stead-
ied herself against a lamp-post, and
said, with the whine coming back into
her voice, 'What d'ye want to know for?'
'I'll see that you get there all right,' said
Belden. The woman laughed again.
She took her hand away from the lamp-
post, and began an effort to walk on
without replying; but in an instant she
swayed, and, had not Belden jumped
toward her and put an arm about her
shoulders, would have fallen.

"She cursed feebly. 'Tell me where you live?' Belden persevered. His voice was harsher and almost a command. She stammered out more sneering evasions; then she flung out the name of the dismal street where she had such residence as that sort ever has. What do you suppose that man Belden did? Hailed a cab, put the woman in, and got in after her. Simply shouted a hasty good-night to me, and drove off. Well,— that's where it all began." Stanley stopped, got up, and walked over to the wall, pressing a button that showed there.

"But you don't mean to say—" began one of the others, with wonder and incredulity in his tone.

"Oh, yes, I do, though. Russell, take the orders, will you? What'll you men drink—or smoke? I've been talking, and my throat's dry."

The darky waited patiently until the several orders had been given. Then he glided away as noiselessly as he had come.

"There is really where the story, as far as I know it, ends," Stanley went on, after he had cooled his throat a little, "The other end of it came to me from Belden the other day. 'Got anything to do Thursday evening?' he asked me. We had been talking of dry-point etching. I told him I thought not. 'Then will you help me jump off?' he went on. Then the whole scene of that winter-night flashed back to me in a sort of wave. I felt, before he answered my question for further information, what his answer would be. 'Yes,' he said, 'it's the same girl. I know her better than I did. Her's is a sad case; very sad. I'm lifting her up out of it.' I didn't say anything, he hadn't asked my opinion. As between man and man there was nothing for me to cavil at; I was invited to a friend's wedding, that was all. I went. I was the only other person present, barring the old German minister that Belden fished out from some dark corner. It was the queerest proceeding! Belden had brought the girl up into a righteous neighborhood some months ago, it seemed; had been paying her way; the neighbors thought she was a person of some means, I suppose. He introduced me to her on the morning of his wedding-day; I think she remembered me, although she has caught manners enough from Belden or her past to conceal what she felt. And so—they were married."

"My God!" groaned Vanstruther, "what an awful thing to do! Lifting her up out of it, does he say? No! He's bringing himself down to it! That's what it always ends in. Always. Oh, I've known cases! Every man thinks he is going to succeed where the others have failed. For they have failed, there is no doubt about that! Look at the case of Gripler, the Elevated magnate!—he did that sort of thing, and the world says and does the same old thing it has always done—sneers a little, and cuts her! He is having the most magnificent house in all Gotham built for himself, I understand, and they are going to move there, but do you suppose for a minute they will ever get into the circle of the elect? Not in a thousand years! Don't misunderstand me: I'm not considering merely the society of the 'society column,' I'm thinking of society at large, the entire human body, the mass of individuals scripturally enveloped in the phrase 'thy neighbor.' The taint never fades; a surface gloss may hide the spot, but some day it blazons itself to the world again in all it's unpleasantness. Take this case of our friend Belden. We, who sit here, are all men who know the world we live in; we will treat Belden himself as we have always done. We will even argue, in that exaggerated spirit of broadness that might better be called laxness, typical of our time, that the man has done a braver thing than ourselves had courage for had the temptation come to us. We will acknowledge that his motive was a good one. He honestly believes that he will educate the girl into the higher life. He thinks the past can be sunk into the pit of forgetfulness; but there is no pit deep enough to hide the past. We will say that he is putting into action what the rest of the radicals continually vapor about; the equal consideration, in matters of morality, of man and woman. He is remembering that a man, we argue, should in strict ethics demand of a woman no more than himself can bring. But, mark my words, the centuries have been wiser than we knew. It is ordained that the man who shall take to wife a woman that has what the world meaningly call 'a past,' shall see the ghost of that past shaking the piece of his house for ever and ever."

There was silence for a few moments. Beyond the curtains, someone came in and threw himself down on the sofa. Marsboro, looking vaguely out at window, said, somewhat irrelevalantly, "I suppose that will be the end of the Sunday evening seances?"

"Oh, I don't know," said Stanley. "If I know anything about Belden, I shall not be surprised if he asks us all up there again one of these evenings. He has lived so long in Free-and-easy-dom that no thought of what people call 'the proprieties' will ever touch him."

"Heigh!" Vanstruther stretched himself reflectively. "It's a queer life a man leads, a queer life! God send us all easy consciences!"

"Don't be pathetic!" Stanley frowned. "The life is generally of our own choosing, and if we play the game we should pay the forfeits. Besides which, it is one of the few things I believe in, that the man who has tasted of sin, and in whose mouth the bitters of revulsion have corroded, is the only one who can ever safely be called good. It is different with a woman. If once she tastes— there's an end of her! Oh, I know very well that we never think this way at first. At first—when we are very young—we think there is nothing in the world so delightful as being for ever and ever as white as the driven snow; then Life sends his card, we make his acquaintance, he introduces us to some of his fastest friends, and we, h'm, begin to change our views a little. In accordance with the faint soiling that is gradually covering up the snowy hues of our being, the strictness of our opinions on the matter of whiteness relaxes notably. Arm in arm with Life, we step slowly down the ladder. Then, if we are in luck, there is a reaction, and we go up again—so far!—only so far, and never any further; if we are particularly fond of Life, we are likely to get very far down indeed; and the end is that Life bids us farewell of his own accord. That is the history of a modern man of the world."

"I believe you are right," said Marsboro, "I know, in my own case at least, that I can remember distinctly how beautiful my young ideal was. But Life is jealous of ideals; he shatters them with a single whiff of experience. And it happened as you just now said: as I descended, my ideals descended. I only hope—he sighed, half in jest, half in earnest,—"that I will begin the upward climb and succeed in winning up."

"Ah, assented Stanley, "that is always the interesting problem. Which it will be: the elevator with the index pointing to 'Up' or the one destined 'Down.' You needn't look so curiously at me, Van, I know what you are wondering. Well you can rest easy in the assurance I give you: the nether slopes are beckoning to me. I became aware of it long ago, reconciled moreover. I live merely for the moment. My senses must amuse me until there is nothing left of them; that is all. But look here: don't think there is no reverse to the medal.

I have, fate knows, my moments of being horrified at myself. It is, I presume, at the times when the ghost of my conscience comes to ask why it was murdered." He appeared to be concentrating all his attention on the ashes at the end of his cigarette. "Why, don't you know that there is no longer any meaning for me in any of those words: honor, and truth, and virtue? I have no standards, except my digestion, and my nerves. I don't mistreat my wife simply because it would come back to me in a thousand little annoyances that would grate on my nerves." He sipped slowly at the glass by his side. "And I'm not worse than some other men!"

"True. All of which is a pity. But we've got off the subject. The villainy of ourselves is too patent a proposition. The question is, by what right we continue to expect of the women we marry that which they dare not expect of us.

"Are you the mouthpiece of the New Woman? Well, the Creator made man king, and the laws of physiology cannot be twisted to suit the New Woman. For it is, in essentials, unfortunately a question of physiological consequences. Wherefore, suppose we stop the argument. This is not a medical congress!"

Stanley went over to the desk where the periodicals lay, and picking one up, began, with a cigarette in his mouth, to let his eyes rest on the printed pages.

"Will you go, if you're asked?" Marsboro said, presently.

"I?" Stanley looked up carelessly. "Certainly. As far as I'm concerned a man may marry the devil and all his angels. But I wouldn't take my wife or my sister."

Vanstruther laughed dryly. "If women were to apply the tit-for-tat principle," he said, "what terribly small visiting lists most of us fellows would have!"

But Stanley disdained further discussion, and the other men got up to go. When they had passed beyond the curtains Stanley laid down the paper he had been reading, and smiled to himself. He was wondering why he had been led into this waste of breath. A man's life was a man's life, and what was the use of cavilling at facts! The only thing to do was to take life lightly and to let nothing matter. Also, one must amuse oneself! If the manner of the amusement was distasteful or hurtful to others, why—so much the worse for the others!

So musing, Laurence Stanley passed into a light slumber, and dreamed of impossible virtues.

But Dick Lancaster, who, from the sofa beyond the curtains, had heard all of this conversation, did not dream of pleasant things that night. In fact, he spent a white night. Like a flood the horrors of self-revelation had come upon him at sound of those arguments and dissections; he saw himself as he was, compared with what he had been; he shuddered and shivered in the grip of remorse.

In the white light of shame he saw whither the wish to taste of life had led him; he realized that something of that hopeless corruption that Stanley had spoken of was already etched into his conscience. Oh, the terrible temptation of all those shibboleths, that told us that we must live while we may! He felt, now that he had seen how deep was the abyss below him, that his feet were long since on the decline, and that from a shy attempt at worldliness he had gone on to what, to his suddenly re-awakened conscience, constituted dissoluteness.

To the man of the world, perhaps, his slight defections from the puritanic code would have seemed ridiculously vague. But, he repeated to himself with quickened anguish, if he began to consider things from the standpoint of the world, he was utterly lost; he would soon be like those others.

He got up and opened the window of his bed-room. Below him was the hum of the cable; a dense mist obscured the electric lights, and the town seemed reeking with a white sweat. He felt as if he were a prisoner. He began to feel a loathing for this town that had made him dispise himself so much. The roar of it sounded like a wild animal's.

Then a breeze came and swept the mist away, and left the streets shining with silvery moisture. Lights crept out of the darkness, and the veil passed from the stars. The wild animal seemed to be smiling. But the watcher at the window merely shrank back a little, closing the window. Fascinating, as a serpent; poisonous as a cobra! The glitter and glamour of society; the devil-may-care fascinations of Bohemia; they had lured him to such agony as this!

Such agony? What, you ask, had this young man to be in agony about? He was a very nice young man—all the world would have told you that! Ah, but was there never a moment in your lives, my dear fellow-sinners—you men and women of the world—when it came to your conscience like a sword-thrust, that the beautiful bloom of your youth and innocence was gone from you forever and that ever afterward there would be a bitter memory or a bitterer forgetfulness? And was that not agony? Ah, we all hold the masks up before our faces, but sometimes our arms tire, and they slip down, and then how haggard we look! Perhaps, if we had listened to our consciences when they were quicker, we would not have those lines of care upon our faces now. You say you have a complexion and a conscience as clear as the dew? Ah, well, then I am not addressing you, of course. But how about your neighbors? Ah, you admit—? Well, then we will each of us moralize about our neighbor. It is so much pleasanter, so much more diverting!

CHAPTER X

WITH the coming of morning, Lancaster shook himself out of his painful reveries, and decided that he must escape from this metropolitan prison, if for ever so short a time. He would go out into the country, home. He would go where the air was pure, and all life was not tainted. He walked to a telegraph office and sent a dispatch to his mother, telling of his coming.

Then he went for a walk in the park. Now that he had made up his mind to get out of this choking dungeon for a while he felt suddenly buoyant, refreshed. He tried to forget Stanley and the Imperial Theatre, and all other unpleasant memories of that sort. Some of the park policemen concluded that this was a young man who was feeling very cheerful indeed—else, why such fervid whistling?

When he got to his studio he found some people waiting for him. They had some commercial work for him to do. He shook his head at all of them.

"I'm going out of town for a week," he said, "and I can do nothing until I return. If this is a case of 'rush' you'll have to take it somewhere else."

He turned the key in the door with a wonderful feeling of elation, and the pinning of the small explanatory notice on his door almost made him laugh aloud. He thought of the joy that a jail bird must feel when he sees the gates opening to let him into the free world. No more elevated roads, no more cable cars, no more clanging of wheels over granite, no more deafening shouts of newsboys; no more tortuous windings through streets crowded with hurrying barbarians; no more passing the bewildering glances of countless handsome women; no more—town!

There was a train in half an hour. He

bought his ticket and strolled up and down the platform. He wondered how the dear old village would look. He had been away only a little over a year, and yet, how much had happened in that short time! Then he smiled, thinking of the intangible nature of those happenings. There was nothing,—nothing that would make as much as a paragraph in the daily paper. Yet how it had changed him, this subtle flow of soul-searing circumstances! It was of such curious woof that modern life was made; so rich in things that in themselves were dismally commonplace and matters of course, and yet in total exerted such strong influences; so rich, too, in crime and casuality, that, though served up as daily dishes, yet seemed always far and outside of ourselves!

The novel he purchased to while away the hours between the town and Lincolnville confirmed his thoughts in this direction. It was one of the modern pictures of "life as it is." There was nothing of romance, hardly any action; it was nearly all introspection and contemplations of the complexity of modern existence. The story bored him immensely, and yet he felt that it was a voice of the time. It was hard to invest today with romance.

Was it, he wondered, a real difference, or was it merely the difference in the point of view? Perhaps there was still romance abroad, but our minds had become too analytical to see the picture of it?—too much engaged in observing the quality of the paint?

His mother was waiting for him at the station. It was pleasant to see how proud she was of this tall young son of hers, and how wistfully she looked deep into his eyes. "You're looking pale, Dick," she said, holding him at the stretch of her arms. "And your eyes look like they needed sleep."

Dick gave a little forced laugh and patted his mother's hand.

"Yes, I guess you're right mother. I need a little fresh air and a rest."

"Ah, you shall have both, my boy. And now tell me all you've been doing up there in that big place."

They walked down to the little house wherein Dick had first seen the light of this world. He looked taller than ever beside the little woman who kept looking him over so wistfully. He told her many things, but he felt that he was talking to her in a language that was rusty on his lips, the language of the country, of simplicity and truth. The language of the world, in which his tongue was now glib, would be so full of mysteries to this sweet mother of his that he must needs eschew it for the nonce. It was a small thing, but he felt it as an evidence of the changes that had been wrought in him.

He told her of his work, of his career. Of the *Torch*, of his subsequent renting of a studio, and free-lance life. Yes, he was making money. He was independent; he had his own hours; work came to him so readily that he was in a position to refuse such as pleased him least. But, he sighed, it was all in

black-and-white, so far. Paint loomed
up, as before, merely as a golden dream.
In illustrating and decorating, using
black-and-white mediums, that was
where the money lay, and he supposed
he would have to stick to that for a
time. But he was saving money for a
trip abroad.

They talked on and on until nearly
midnight. He asked after some of his
old acquaintances; he listened patiently
to his mother's gentle gossip and tried
to feel interested.

"The Wares are back," explained
Mrs. Lancaster.

"Ah," Dick looked up quickly. "Does
Dorothy look well?"

"I don't think so, though I'm bound
I hadn't the courage to tell her so to her
face. She looks just like you do, Dick,
—kinder fagged out."

"Yes. They say traveling is hard
work. And her mother?"

"Oh, she's about the same as usual.
Looks stouter, maybe."

"I must get over and call there, before I get back to town," he said, reflectively. "Well, mother, I suppose I'm
keeping you up beyond your regular
time. I'm a trifle tired, too. So good-
night."

He kissed her and passed up stairs to
his old room. There were the same
pictures that he had decorated the walls
with a few years ago. He smiled; they
were, fortunately, very crude compared
to the work he was doing now. When
all was dark, he lay awake for a long
time, drinking in the deep silence of the

place. He could hear the chirrup of the crickets over in the meadows, and from far over the western hills came the deep boom of a locomotive's whistle. The incessant roar of the town, in which even the shrillest of individual noises are swallowed into one huge conglomerate, was utterly gone. He could hear the wind slightly swaying the branches; the deep blue of the star-spotted sky was full of a caressing silence. The peace of it all soothed him, and ushered him into deep, refreshing sleep.

The sun touched him early in the morning, and seeing the beauty of the dawning day, he dressed quickly and went quietly down stairs and out, for a stroll about the dear old village. He passed the familiar houses, smiling to himself. He thought of all the quaint and queer characters in a little place of this sort. Presently he left the region of houses and passed into the woods that were beginning to blush at the approach of their snow-clad bridegroom. The picture of the sun rising over the fringe of trees, gilding the browned leaves with a burnish that blazed and sparkled, filled him with artistic delight. He said to himself that after he had been abroad, and after his hand was grown cunning in colors, he would ask for no better subject than these October woods of the West. He sat down on the log of a tree and watched the golden, crescent lamp of day. He had forgotten the town utterly, for the moment, and for the moment he was happy.

But the sun's progress warned him

that it was time to start back to the house. With swinging stride he passed over the highway, over the slopes that led to the village. Suddenly he heard his named called, and turning, saw a tall figure hastening toward him.

It was Mr. Fairly, the minister.

"My dear Dick," he said, shaking the young man's hand, "I am rejoiced to see you. We have heard of you, of course; we have heard of you. But that is not seeing you. Let me look at you!"

Dick smiled. "I've grown, I believe."

"Yes. In stature and wisdom, I dare say. But—" He sliped his arm within Dick's, and walked with him silently for a few minutes. "The town," he went on, "has a brand of its own, and all that live there, wear it." They passed a boy going to school. "Look at that youngster. Isn't he bright-eyed!" A farm wagon drove by, the farmer and his wife sitting side by side on the springless seat. "Did you get t h e sparkle of their faces?" said the minister. "Their skins were tanned a n d rough, no doubt, but their eyes were clear. Now, Dick, your eyes have been reading many pages of the Book of Knowledge and they are tired. I know, my boy, I know. We buzz about the electric arc-light till we singe our wings, and then, perhaps, we are wiser. Have you been singeing your's?"

"Not enough, I'm afraid. The fascination is still there. Sometimes it is the fascination of danger, sometimes of repulsion; but it is always fascination."

"Ah, so you have got to the repulsion!" The minister spoke softly, almost as if to himself. "And you no longer think the world is all beautiful, and sometimes you wonder whether virtue is a dream or a reality? I know, I know! And sometimes you wish you were blind again, as once you were; and you want to wipe away the taste of the fruit of knowledge?"

Dick said nothing.

"Those who chose the world as their arena," the minister went on, "must suffer the world's jars and jeers. The world is a magnet that draws all the men of courage; it sucks their talents and their virtues and spews them forth, as often as not into the waters of oblivion. To swim ashore needs wonderful strength! Here in the calmer waters we are but tame fellows; we miss most of the prizes, but, we also miss the dangers. Perhaps, some day, Dick, you'll come back to us again?"

"I don't know. Perhaps. But I don't think so. That other taste is bitter, perhaps, but it holds one captive. And I'm changed, you see; the old things that delighted me once are stale, and I need the perpetual excitation of the town's unceasing changes. The town is a juggernaut with prismatic wheels."

They had nearly reached the minister's house.

"I haven't preached to you, have I Dick?"

Dick looked at the minister quickly. There was a sort of wistfulness behind the eye-glasses, and a half smile beneath the waving mustache.

"No. I wish you would!"

"Ah, Dick, I can't! I'm not competent. You're in one world, and I'm in another. Too many make the mistake that they can live in the valleys and yet tell the mountaineers how to climb. But, Dick, whatever you do, keep your self-respect! In this complex time of ours, circumstances and comparisons alter nearly everything, and one sometimes wonders whether b-a-d does not, after all, spell good; but self-respect should stand against all confusions! Goodbye, Dick. Remember we're all fond of you! I go to a convention in one of the neighboring towns tonight, and I won't see vou again before you go back. Goodbye!"

Dick carried the picture of the kindly, military-looking old face with him for many minutes. If there were more such ministers! He recalled some of the pale, cold clergymen he had met at various houses in town, and remembered how repellant their haughty assumption of superiority has been to him. He was still musing over his dear old friend's counsel, when he noticed that he was approaching the house where the Wares lived. There was the veranda, blood red with it's creeper-clothing, and full of memories for him.

He began to walk slowly as he drew nearer. He was thinking of the last time that he had seen Dorothy Ware. He recalled, with a queer smile, her parting words: 'Goodbye, Dick, be good!' He realized that the Dick of that day and the Dick of today were

two very differing persons. And she,
too, doubtless, would no longer be the
Dorothy Ware he once had known.
Something of fierce hate toward the
world and fate came to him as he
thought of the way of human plans and
planning were truthlessly canceled by
the decrees of change. Had he been
good? Bah, the thought of it made him
sneer. If these memories were not to
be driven away he would presently settle down into determined, desperate
melancolia.

The conflict, in this man, was always
between the intrinsic good and the
veneer of vice that the world puts on.
In most men the veneer chokes everything else. When those men read this,
if they ever do, they will wonder why
in the world this young man was tor-
turing himself with fancies? But the
men whose outer veneer has not yet
choked the soul will remember and understand.

Dorothy Ware was on the veranda,
gathering some of the vine's dead leaves
when Dick's step sounded on the wood-
en sidewalk. As he saw her, his face
lit up. He never noticed that the flush
on her face was of another sort.

She smiled at him.

"How do you do, Dick? Come up
and shake hands."

Then they stood and looked at each
other silently for an instant. We're
both a little older," said Dick. "But I
suppose we have so much to talk about
that we'll have to make this a very passing meeting. Besides, mother's waiting

for me; I've been for a morning walk, you see. You'll be at the great and only Fair, I suppose?"

"Oh, yes; I've almost forgotten how it looks. I do hope they will have a fine day for it."

Miss Ware looked after him wistfully. She thought of the thunderstorm in the forest at Schandau, and sighed.

CHAPTER XI

THE first day of the County Fair was hardly eventful. The farmers were busy bringing in their exhibits of stock and produce, and arranging them properly for the inspection of the judges. It is all merely by way of preparation for the big day, the day on which the trotting and running races take place.

Fortunately, it was a cloudless day. Shortly after sunrise clouds of dust began to fill the air. All the roads leading fairwards are filled all morning with every sort and condition of vehicle. Farmers come from the farthest bounderies of the county, bringing their families; the young men bringing their "best girls." This volume of traffic soon reduces the road-bed to a fine, powdery dust, that rises, mist-like and obscures the face of the earth and sky.

Soon the presence of the Fair is felt in the village itself, and the "square" resounds to the cries of the omnibus drivers soliciting fares. "All aboard, now, for the Fair Grounds, only ten cents!" So runs the invitation yelled from half a dozen lusty, though dusty throats. For this occasion every livery stable in the place brings out all the ramshackle conveyances it has. Everything on wheels is pressed into service. Like Christmas, the great day of the County Fair, comes but once a year, and must be made the most of. Few people are going to walk on so dusty a day as this, so the 'bus drivers ply up and down from seven in the morning until dusk sets in, and the last home-stragglers have left the grounds.

At noon, the highway was become a very sea of dust. Dick had walked down to the "square," and was looking about for a conveyance of some sort when a carriage came up with Mrs. Ware and her daughter inside. Dorothy spoke to the coachman, and then waved a daintily gloved hand at Dick. "Delighted!" said that young man, getting in quickly, and adding, in Mrs. Ware's direction, "This is awfully kind in you!" In that course of the drive there was as little said as possible, because each sentence meant a mouthful of dust.

As they passed through the gates at last, Dick smiled at the dear familiar sight that yet seemed something strange. There was the half-mile track in the open meadow; the ridiculously small grand-stand perched against the western horizon, the acres of sloping ground, shaded by lofty oaks, and covered by a mass of picturesquely rural humanity.

Against the inclosing fence the countless stalls, filled with the show stock of the county. The crowd was surging around the track, the various refreshment booths, the merry-go-rounds, and the spaces where the "fakirs" held forth. The grand-stand was filled to running over. The air was resonant with laughter; with t h e appeals of the "fakirs," with the neighing of the hundreds of horses hitched in every part of the field.

The driver halted his horses as close as possible to get to the centre of attraction, the race-track. Then, the horses turning restive, Mrs. Ware decided to get out and go over to the dairy-booth, and see some of her friends from the farms. Dorothy and Dick accompanied her, but had soon exhausted the attractions of the booth. Mrs. Ware guessed she wouldn't g o with them. They started out into the motley crew of sightseers together.

As they approached the grand-stand again, their ears were assailed with by a number of quaint and characteristic cries. "Right down this way, now, and see the man with the iron jaw! Free exhibition inside every minute! Walk up, walk up, and see the ring-tailed monkey eat his own tail!" The most laughable part of this exuberant invitation was that it had nothing to do with a circus or a dime-museum, it was merely the vocal hall-mark of an ambitious seller of lemonade and candy. It was one of the tricks of the trade.

It caught the fancy of the countryman. It sounded well.

There were other cries, such as: "Here's your chance. Ten shots for a nickel," and "the stick you ring is the stick you gits!" "This way for the great panoramy of Gettysburg, just from Chicago!" "Pink lemo. here, five a glass; peanuts, popcorn!" "The only Californy fruit on the grounds here!" "Ten cents admits you to the quarter-stretch—don't crowd the steps, move on, keep a-moving!" Babel was come again.

The farm-people themselves were a healthy, cheering sight. They were all bent on as much wholesome enjoyment as was possible. It looked as if every man, woman and child in the county was there. They had, most of them, come for the day, eating their meals in their vehicles, or under the trees on the green sward. The meadow was a blaze of color. The dresses of the women, with the color-note in them exaggerated in rustic love of brightness, gave the scene a touch of picturesqueness. The white tents of the various booths, the greenleaf trees, the glaring yellow sun over head, and the dust-white track stretching out in the gray mist of heat and dust made a picture of cheer and warmth.

A cheering from the grand-stand. A trotting heat is being run, and the horses have been around for the first time. It is not like the big circuit meeting, this, and Dick thought with something of gladness that the absence of a betting-shed left the scene an unalloyed charm.

Everybody thinks himself competent to speak of the merits of the horses. "He ain't got that sorrel bitted right," declares one authority. "He'll push the bay mare so she'll break on the turn; there—watch her—what 'd I tell you!" triumphs another. A third utters the disgusted sentiment that "Dandy Dan 'd win ef he wuz driv right." And so on. Dick and Dorothy smile at each other as they listen. There is nothing pleasanter in the world than a silent jest as jointure.

Then there comes a rush of dust up the track, a clatter of hoofs over the "stretch," a whirl of wheels, cheers from the crowd and the heat is lost and won.

And so the day wears on, and the program dwindles. There are several trotting races, a pacing event, a running race, and some bicycle exhibitions. The day is to be topped off with a balloon ascent, the balloonist, a woman, being billed to descend, afterward, by way of a parachute.

But to neither of these two spectators did the events of the program seem the most interesting of the displays. It was the country people themselves that had the most of quaint charms. Miss Dorothy Ware was become so saturated with the polish of cosmopolitan views, and the manners caught from extensive travel, that these scenes, once so familiar and natural, now struck her as very strange and extraordinary. In Dick the air of the metropolis had so keyed him up to the quick, unwholesome pleasures

of the urban mob that this breath of
country holiday filled him with a pleasant sense of rest. Never again could he
be as these were, but he could, in a far-
off, dreamy way, still appreciate their
primitive emotions. They were all so
ingenious, so openly joyful, so gayly
bent on having a good time, these country folk! They strolled about in groups
of young folk, or in couples, or in family parties. She casts a wistful look
toward a fruit-stand; he must go prompt-
ly and buy her something. He bargains
closely; he is mindful, doubtless, of the
fact that there is still the yearning for
the merry-go-round, the phonograph,
and the panorama, to be appeased.

In the West the sun was taking on
the dull red tone of shining, beaten
bronze. The haze of dust began to lift,
mist-wise, up against the shadowgirt
horizon. From thousands of lips there
presently issues a long drawn "Ah-h!"
and the unwieldy mass of a balloon is
seen to rise up over the meadow. A
damsel in startling, grass-green tights
floats in mid-air upheld by the resisting
parachute, and drops earthward to the
safe seclusion of a neighboring pasture.
Vehicles are unhitched; there are some
moments of wild shouting and maneuver-
ing, and then the stream of humanity
and horses pours out into the dusty
road, and in a little while the fair
grounds are merely a place for the ghosts
of the things that were.

When it was all over, when he had
said goodbye to Miss Ware and her
mother, a sense of loneliness came over

Dick, and he sank into one of those moody states that nowadays invariably meant torment. He could not remember to have talked to Dorothy of anything save commonplace and obvious things, and yet with every glance of her eye, every tone of her voice, the old glamour that he had felt aforetime had come upon him again. She was no longer the same, he had observed so much; the girlish exuberance and forthrightness had given way to a more subdued manner, a fine, but somewhat colorless polish. Something, too, of the sparkle seemed to have gone from her; her smile had much of sadness.

It flashed over him that never once had either of them referred to the words with which they once had parted. Had it been his fault, or hers? Once, she had let him hope, had she not? He remembered the dead words, but he smiled at the dim tone that yon whole picture took in his memory. It was as if it had all happened to someone else. Well,—perhaps it had; certainly he was separated by leagues of too well remembered things from that other self, the self that had said to a girl, once, "Dorothy, will you wish me luck?"

But in spite of the changes in them both, Dick felt that her charm for him was potent with a new fervor. He could not define it; it seemed a halo that surrounded her, in his eyes at least. The sardonic recesses of his memory flashed to him the echo of his foolish words to Mrs. Stewart, at the opera. "Oh, damn the past," he muttered, hotly. He would begin all over again, he would atone for those pretty steps aside; he would pin his faith to the banner of his love for Dorothy. For he felt that he did love this girl. He longed for her; she seemed to personify a harbor of refuge, a comfort; he felt that if he could go to her, and tell her everything, and feel her hand upon his forehead, her smile, and the touch of her hand would wipe away all the ghost.y cobwebs of his memory, of his past, and leave him looking futureward with stern resolves for white, and happy, wholesome days.

Surely it would be madly foolish to let a Past spoil a Future!

He saw the grin upon the face of Sophistry, and set his lips. No, there were no excusing circumstances; he had gone the way of the world, because that way was easy and pleasant. Only his weakness was to blame.

"She is as far above me," he said, before he went to sleep that night, "as the stars. But—we always want the stars!"

As for Miss Ware, it need only be chronicled that she was very quiet and abstracted that evening, so that her mother was prompted to remark that "Lincolnville don't appear to suit you powerful well, Dorothy." As a matter of fact, the girl was afar off, in thought, and her eyes were bright with tears because of the things she was remembering.

She had loved Dick, on a time. And to realize that never, in all time, would her conscience permit her to satisfy that love—that was bitter, very bitter.

$$\text{\&}$$

CHAPTER XII

WINTER was coming over the town. The gripmen of the cable cars were muffled to their noses in heavy buffalo coats, and the pedestrians were heralded by the white steam that testified to the frostiness of the air. The newspaper boys performed "break downs" on the corners for the mere warmth thereof, and the beggars and tramps presented a more blue-nosed, frost-bitten appearance than usual.

Everybody was in town once more. The hills, the seaside and the watering places had all given up their summer captives, and the metropolis held them all. The Tremonts were returned from Europe. The opera season, promising better entertainment than ever, had lured many of the wealthier folk from the country, for the winter at least. Among these were the Wares. It was a fashion steadily increasing in favor, this of living in town the winter over, and retiring to rusticity for the dog days. With the Wares it was not yet become a fashion; it was merely in accordance with Dorothy's wish to hear the opera and the concert season that the move townward was made.

Mrs. Annie McCallum Stewart's little "evenings" were more popular than ever. There seemed a positive danger that she would become known as the possessor of a "salon" and have a society reporter describe a representative gathering of her satellites. On this particular evening the carriages drove up to the house and drove off again without intermission all the evening. People had a habit of coming there before the theatre, or after; of staying ten minutes or two hours, just as their fancy, or Mrs. Stewart might dictate.

One of the latest to arrive was Dick Lancaster. It was his first appearance there that season. He had only come because he had heard that Dorothy Ware was to be there. He hardly looked as well as usual. He had been working very hard, making up for the time lost in the country. His cheek-bones stood out a trifle prominently, and his eyes were tired.

Mrs. Stewart proffered him the tips of her fingers, shaking her head at him with mockery of a frown.

"You ought to be introduced to me again," she said.

"I've been tremendously busy."

"Ah, you plagiarist! The sins that the word 'busy' is made to cover! People escape debts, and calls, and engagements, nowadays, by simply flourishing the magic word 'busy.'" She broke off, and began to look at him steadily over the top of her fan. Then she went on in a very low voice, "And have you found out how one's youth is lost in town?"

"You're cruel," he murmured.

"Not I. But there, go in and talk to the others. There are lots of people you haven't met before, and there are some pretty girls. Go in, and enjoy yourself if you can. And perhaps, if you find time, and I think of it again, I shall ask you to introduce me to your new self.

"I've never been introduced to that new self yet, *egomet ipse.*"

He found two arch-enemies, Mrs. Tremont and Miss Leigh, conversing with cheerless enthusiasm. "I heard of you a good deal while I was abroad," said Mrs. Tremont, after greetings had been exchanged. Dick bowed, and looked a question.

"It was Mr. Wooton mentioned you," Mrs. Tremont went on, pompously. "We met in Germany. A charming man!" She said it with the air of one conferring a knighthood.

Dick was wondering how many times a day a woman like this one managed to be sincere. Then he said, "Miss Tremont is well, I trust?"

"Yes. She's here somewhere." She lifted her lorgnette deliberately and gazed toward the piano, "Who is that playing?" she asked.

"Mrs. Stewart herself," said Miss Leigh.

"Dear me! I didn't know she played. I must go and congratulate her." • She moved off with severe dignity.

Miss Leigh laughed as she watched the expression on Dick's face.

"Do you believe in heridity?" he asked.

"Yes, and no. Not in this case, if that's what you mean. Miss Tremont is far too clever. Do you know," she went on, with slow distinctness, "that you are changed."

He made a movement of impatience. "I have heard nothing but that all evening," he declared. "Simply because the town had put it's brand on me, whether I wished it or no, am I to be forever upbraided?" There was both petulence and pathos in his voice.

"H'm," she said, "you still have all your old audacity. But I don't think it is anything but genuine interest in you that prompts such remarks."

"You once said something about being genuine. You said it was pathetic. Now I know why that is so true. The pathos comes after one has lost the genuineness.

"Yes, but when one does nothing but think and think, and brood and brood, the pathos turns bathos. The thing to do is to laugh!"

"Is that why there is so much flippancy?"

"No doubt. Tragedy evokes flippancy and comedy starts tears."

"You are a very fountain of worldly paradoxes. Where do you get them all from?"

"From my enemies. I love my enemies, you know, for what I can deprive them of. That's right, leave me just when I'm getting brilliant! Go and talk to Miss Ware about the rich red tints of the Indian summer leaves and the poetry in the gurgle of the brook.

Go on, it will be like a breath of fresh air after the dismal gloom of my conversation!" She got up, laughing, and added, in a voice that he had not heard before, "Go in and win! Your eyes have told your secret."

She moved off, and he saw Dorothy Ware coming toward him. He noticed how delightfully she seemed to fit into this scene; how charmingly at ease and how natural she looked. Her color was not as fresh as it once had been; but he remembered how popular she had at once become in town, and that her life was now a very whirl of dances and receptions and festive occasions of that sort. He had hardly shaken hands when Mrs. Tremont and her daughter approached from different directions. They were both, they declared, so perfectly delighted to see Miss Ware again.

Mrs. Stewart sailed majestically up to them at this juncture, and bore Lancaster away in triumph. He heard Mrs. Tremont asking Dorothy, as he moved away, "And how's your poor, dear mother?" Then he found himself being introduced to a personage with a Vandyke beard.

"Ah," said the personage, with some show of interest, "you're an artist? Now, tell me, frankly, why do you Western artists never treat Western subjects?" And then Dick found himself floundering about in a sea of argument with this personage. Afterwards, when the agony was over, he discovered that it was the author, Mr. Wreath, who had thus been catechizing him. It was noised

about the world that Mr. Wreath was a
monomaniac on the subect of realism.
Dick remembered wishing he had caught
the man's name at the introduction.

In the meanwhile Miss Tremont stood
talking to Dorothy Ware in a dim corner
of the room. There was a small table
near them, and upon it were scattered
portfolios of photographs.

"Do you ever hear of Mr. Wooton?"
Miss Tremont asked, smiling sweetly.

Dorothy gave a little start, and a flush
touched her cheek.

"No," she said tonelessly.

"He's a very clever man," persisted
Miss Tremont. "I congratulate you."
She smiled meaningly.

"I'm sure I don't know what you
mean?" Dorothy's eyes flashed and her
fingers toyed nervously with the photographs.

"If I were an expert photographer I
could show you what I mean instantly.
Speech is so clumsy!"

Dorothy still looked at her blankly,
though she felt her heart beating with
accelerated speed.

"From what I saw at Schandau," the
other went on coldly, "I should say it
was time to announce the engagement."

Dorothy gripped the little table with
a tight clasp. Bending over, as if to ex-
amine the pictures, she felt waves of
heat and cold follow each other over
her cheeks and forehead. Her breath
seemed to choke. How warm the room
was! She longed for a breath of fresh
air. She would go and tell her mother
that she wanted to have the carriage

called at once. But there was her mother talking busily with Mrs. Tremont. And there, beyond, was Dick.

Something very like tears came to the borders of her eyes, as Miss Dorothy Ware looked at, and thought of Dick. He had loved her, and she— Ah, well, that was all over now! Even had she been able to compound with her own conscience, Miss Tremont had effectually barred the way to—ah, to everything! There was Miss Tremont talking, now, to Mr. Wreath and to Dick. Surely the girl would not dare—but no, that was absurd!

Fortunately, Miss Leigh, noticing Dorothy's solitude, decided, just then, that she would go and talk to the girl, which succeeded in diverting Dorothy's mind from unpleasant thoughts.

At the other end of the room the various groups were constantly changing. Above the chatter one could hear the strains of music that floated in from the music-room. Miss Tremont having finally succeeded in luring Mr. Wreath on to a discussion of his own peculiar theory of the art of fiction, Dick left them and strolled into the conservatory. He wanted to be alone. He had been suffering more than ever before from such accute pain as afflicts each individual soul that submits to drowning itself in the meaningless chatter of society. As he himself put it, with something like an oath of disgust, "I've been listening to people I don't care a pin about; hearing rubbish and talking rubbish!" The real key to his feeling of disgust, however, was in the fact that his opportunities to a confidential talk with Miss Ware had all been ruthlessly killed.

"A nice way to contribute to the general entertainment!" It was Mrs. Stewart herself. She was shaking her fan at him. "Don't get up!" she went on, "I want to talk to you." She scrutenized him. You don't look cheerful!"

"I'm not," he said curtly.

"Remorse?"

"No. Remorse is the divine right of cowards and gourmands. Mine is merely a case of weariness.

"With your own sweet self to blame. I know the feeling. You've been thinking, or, rather, you think you have been thinking. And when one is in that state, everything goes against the grain. Even such a galaxy as that!" She waved her fan to the direction of the inner rooms, and a smile of mischief curled her mouth. "What do you think of this year's crop of lions?"

"Bah!" he scorned viciously, with all the bitterness of the man knocking at the closed portals. "Who was it that first gave your friend Clarence Miller the idea that he was a novelist? His wife, I suppose. When a man's single his follies are suggested by the devil; when he's married, by his wife. I suppose she wants her husband to equal the notoriety attained by her brother-in-law, the composer of 'Rip Van Winkle' and other comic operas that society flocks to listen to. It's a great pity that art and literature happen to be the thing this season."

"You're thinking of the real artists and writers, I presume. Well, it is rather hard on them."

"Hard? Why, its death! Think of the author that finds the market glutted with the free-gratis product of the society butterfly's pen. Its enough to create suicides."

"But you can't very well include Mr. Wreath in the free-gratis class?"

"No. But he is a charlatan, for revenue only. He has so many fads that they stud his conversation as barnacles cover a rock. He is a trumpeter of theories. Oh, I don't deny that he writes well! But he is not satisfied with that, unfortunately; he must needs preach, and the man who preaches about his art is a dispiriting spectacle."

"Dear, dear! What a change! It used to be that we others said all the cutting things, while you listened in awe and trembling; now it is you that uses the edge tools of language. You have beaten us at our own game." Mrs. Stewart dropped her voice a little, and sighed. "But you have lost as much as you have gained, have you not?"

He nodded silently. "The world is a usurer that lends us wisdom if we will but pay our youth as interest. And when we are bankrupt in youth, the wisdom turns to ashes."

"Don't be morbid. It's too fashionable. Cynicism is so cheap nowadays that the poorest Philistine of us all can afford it. The only virtue in optimism, it seems to me, is that it is suffering neglect today; for that reason I may espouse it, merely to avoid the charge of being commonplace. Come, be gay! Laugh! Forget!"

"To forget is to forego one of life's sweetest pains." He laughed mechanically, and got up, offering Mrs. Stewart his arm. "I'm a stupid, morbid fool. My only saving grace is that I know just how big a fool I am." They entered the inner rooms, and Mrs. Stewart, with a smile and a bow, left Dick to talk flatteringly to the musical lion of the town.

Some of the people were already leaving. Dick determined to slip away quietly. But, as he turned to the vestibule, he found himself face to face with Dorothy Ware.

All his gloom vanished. "I've been trying to talk to you all evening," he declared. "I've been wanting to ask you something. I asked you once before. But that seems a very long time ago." He found himself carried away in a whirl of eager enthusiasm and hope. "Dorothy," he said, looking down at her, "there is still hope for me, is there not?"

But in the girl's eyes there was nothing save pain, and shame. She looked away. She played nervously with the lace of her dress.

Blind, man-like, he took it all for shyness. "Only a little hope," he repeated, tenderly. He tried to take her hand.

She shrank away from him in a sort of horror. "No, no," she murmured, in a voice of torture. She did not look him in the face.

Dick stared at her dumbly. Now, at last, he understod her silence, her averted head. He saw the expression that told him she feared to wound him, even though she cared for him not at all.

"Forget me!" she said, and moved away quickly.

He stood, for an instant, looking after her, then he went, moving his lips in a queer, mumbling way, to the vestibule, and asked for his wraps.

As he was leaving the house Dorothy was sinking into a chair by her mother's side. She stared straight out in front of her. When her mother spoke to her she turned slowly around and said, "It's very cold in here." She shivered.

And her mother, knowing that it was as warm as an oven in those rooms, and watching the queer look on her daughter's face, decided the latter was not very well, and must be taken home at once.

❦

CHAPTER XIII

HE went down the steps with his hand clutching the rail with the fervor of a tooth biting on a lip. If it had been daylight the twitching of his eyes and lip-corners would have been peculiarly noticeable.

For some reason or no reason he scorned the sidewalk; the middle of the road presently felt his nervous footfall.

Underneath him he could feel and hear the droning of the cable. Some hundred yards before him he saw the vivid glare that betokened the headlight of an approaching cable-car. For an instant or two he asked himself why he should not continue walking in that direction, in the path of the Juggernaut, and allow himself to be ground into fragments— into the everlasting Forget. Gravely he pondered it: why not? Could the game be worth the candle that was snuffed? And yet, there was something so commonplace, so cheaply melodramatic in that manner of going out that he drew back; he stepped aside and let the dust of the passing car brush him spatteringly. To commit suicide, to choose such a moment for it—a moment that, after all, was but the repetition of a million similar ones—had something so ordinary, so vulgar in it, that after he resisted the thought of it, he shuddered. His lips took on a semblance of smiling.

"What a play for the gallery it would have been!" he thought bitterly.

Presently, as he walked, sobs broke through his lips. The measure of what was lost to him seemed terribly great. All the light of the world was but darkness for him now. What did it all matter now, this world, this life, this aimless race? What was ambition worth, when ambition's cause was gone? Could he take up the dream again, now that waking had brought such pain? Incoherently his mind went back to the moments that had elapsed just before he had left the house, moments that lasted longer than lifetimes. He saw it all again, that scene so indelibly graven on his mental film; he heard those fateful words again and felt their blighting import. His arms went up wildly, with fists clenched, toward the stars, and down again toward the earth like falling hammers, driven with curses.

If anyone had met him at that moment, Dick Lancaster would have been called insane.

Suddenly he stood still, and began to laugh. It was not a pleasant sound, and he himself noticed that it had the discordance of the laugh bred by artifice. He had remembered a sentence that someone had addressed to him, "The thing to do is to laugh !"

So it was. Yes, that was the only armor, the armor of indifference. He walked on, evolving a philosophy of flippancy. Wounded sorely, as he was, he found himself sympathetically wondering whether that flippancy that he once had so despised in his fellow-men and women was not as often a growth of experience as a mask of fashion.

When he reached his room he flung himself on a couch. Outside everything was still. He sent his mind back to the time when he had first entered this town. How void of all suspicion, all cynicism, he was in those days! Experience after experience had left its impress on his wax-like mind and now, with the sliping away of beliefs, the vanishment of idols, the twinges of fate, he found himself at the other extreme, in the mood that laughs at all things, and believes that there is nothing potent save chance.

In that mood he resolved to remain. It was the only one that was no longer unbearable. To attempt the old beliefs were merely to give hostages to disinchantment. He was done now with disinchantment. He would expect nothing, care for nothing. Except to laugh.

But, in the meanwhile, he could no longer bear the scenes and sounds of the town. He cast about for plans. The thought that in one mind at least his flight would look like cowardice did not annoy him; that also was merely a thing to laugh at. The country was not what he wanted. It was not quiet he desired; it was struggle and strife with the dragons of memory and boredom; he wanted new battles to fight, new experiences to harvest—not sensitively, as of old, but coldly, cruelly—in other fields, as far away as possible.

He unlocked his desk and searched for his bank-book. The figures seemed to satisfy him.

"Three thousand," he murmured, "will be enough. I will take a year. I will see everything that my fancy asks for, do everything, be everything. They call it the Old World. Well, it must be able to furnish amusement for me, be it old or young."

He turned to the unfinished sketches, the letters and the other impediments that littered the room. "These shall not hold me a minute," he said. "I want a change of air. I am going to take it. Nor friends, nor promises, nor prospects shall stay me. It's goodbye."

He laughed again, and went out to buy an evening paper, to scan the sailing-lists for the out-going steamers.

CHAPTER XIV

ON one of the hottest days of August, a month by no means the most delightful of Berlin's moods, there sat in the pleasant, shady garden of the restaurant "Zum Kapuziner," facing the Schlossplatz, a tall young man, whose material externals proclaimed him, to the trained eye, either as an Englishman or an American. It is a safe axiom that all the well-dressed people in the German capital are either English or American.

In front of the young man, on the table, were a glass, a bottle of *Mai-trank* and an illustrated paper. But the young man was not regarding any of these things, but kept his eyes to an observance of the passers-by. This seemed to amuse him, for from time to time he smiled softly.

It was certainly a pleasant spot. In front there stretched the broad, paved square that gave to the Old Castle of the first German Emperors on the left, to the royal stables on the right, and beyond, straight ahead, gave a glimpse of the quaint, old-fashioned architecture of the "*Alte Stadt*." For the Schloss-platz marks the limits of the newer portion of Berlin; beyond the bridge everything is the real Berlin, the Berlin untouched by the triumphant splendors that came after '71, the Berlin that knows but little of the passing stranger and the ways to despoil him. And that was why Dick Lancaster had chosen the spot. The passers-by were not at all cosmopolitan; there was little of that mixture of all races, all garbs, all voices, that was to be seen and heard on the "*Linden.*" These were the real Berliners.

In the months that lay between this day and the day on which Lascaster had first felt the soil of Europe under his foot, there had come to him many experiences, many amusements. He had accepted all things. Unfettered by any restraints he had probed all the novelties that presented themselves. He had lived in alternating fevers of discriminations and hard work. For all these new aspects of life and living filled him with the old, dear mania to create. He found himself inspired by the very overflow of his sensations. From long draughts of enjoyment he plunged into as long fits of artistic energy.

He found, moreover, that the increased tension of his spiritual being put a peculiar force into his pencil. Because it was merely one way of laughter, because he began in a spirit of flippancy, the sketches all succeeded immensely. Fortune began to favor him in artistic ways. In Paris he had made a portfolio full of the most admirable sketches of types. There was a crafty cynicism about his work that gave a fas-

cination to them; something not caricature, but finer. Now he chose as his
subject the traveling millionaire, now
the splendid queen of the boulevard,
now the phantom of the "brasseie," and
now the rag-picker. One day he had
showed some sketches to a man that
had begged permission to glance through
the portfolio, as they sat, in a crowded
cafe, at the same table. The man was
the manager of a famous illustrated
paper. He bought some of the sketches,
and presently there appeared a most astonishingly eulogistic article about this
young American.

People carefully read the name. They
had never heard of him. They looked at
the sketches. That was certainly talent of a significant sort. The other
papers followed suit. The noise of this
discovery went across the channel.
There came to this young man orders
from London, and the newspapers of that
town began to print the most extraordinary inventions, by way of personalities,
about him. The world, now as ever, is
always glad of a new subject. After
that Parisian journal had sounded the
first note, the volume of sound that had
as its burden Lancaster's name, grew
and grew. Of course, there were those
that dissented, that took occasion to flay
this young man's achievements until
there seemed left only a skeleton of
faults. But even that only swelled the
flood.

All the while, his sketches grew in
force and individuality. For, whatever
else his detractors denied him, they ad-

mitted the originality of his style. It had never been done before. Some called it hideous, some grotesque; but all called it new. That was the great point.

He became the fad. The representatives of American newspapers, who had been prompt to cable home reports of the successes of this unheard-of youth, began to attempt to interview him. Whereupon, having by that time exhausted the immediate enjoyments of Paris, he fled abruptly.

His success had at first surprised, then amused him. When, presently, he found that his bank account was swelling most astonishingly, he was more entertained than ever. He laughed— that unpleasant, mirthless laugh. But he felt no duties toward his success. When Paris became tiresome, he had no hesitation about quitting it without leaving an address. For that matter, he did not, himself, know just whither he would go.

His ticket had been taken for Monaco. The life of that place fascinated him no less than that of Paris, when Paris was fresh to him. Day after day he watched the procession that filed to and from the green tables; the princes of the blood, the newest nabobs, the touring Americans, the Russians, the worldlings and half-worldlings of all nations and degrees. He watched the blue of the Mediterranean as a contrast to the blacknesses of humanity that he saw daily.

And then without an accompanying word, he sent a selection of sketches to that Parisian paper whose discovery, so to say, he was. There came another salvo of applause from the world of art. It seemed, so they all said, as if this young man was destined to show such possibilities in black-and-white as had not yet been dreampt of.

From Monaco the wanderer went to Egypt. A white-sailed fishing-smack, anchored in the bay below him, had started the thought in his mind one sunny afternoon, when the attractions of Monte Carlo were beginning to pall. He could afford extravagances now. The fisherman, when he was accosted, had smiled. Yes, he might charter the boat. But where would the gentleman wish to sail to? And it was of Egypt that Dick thought, suddenly, with a longing for the cold silences of the sands, and the pyramids, and the quaking waves of heat. And so the bargain was arranged and to Egypt went the artist.

Thence he swung back to Italy. Then through Switzerland. Everywhere he roved through the corners that his fancy led him to; nowhere did he merely echo the footsteps of the millions of tourists. Sometimes he walked for whole days at a time. Sometimes he went to a petty inn and astonished the host by staying all day in his room and working. Whenever he found his purse suffering unduly through the vagaries of his nomadic fancies, he posted some sketches to such of the Paris or London papers as had been most clamorous for them.

It was, perhaps, just because he cared so little for it all, that this luck was

come to him. In the old days he had
chafed against misfortunes, against
limitations of all sorts; he had declared
that great successes were no longer possible, that everything worth doing had
been done long ago. Now, when he
cared not at all, fortune kissed him.
Which also amused him.

Another man would have laid plans
for the furtherment of this fame, would
have counted the ways and means of
plucking the fruit of success at it's ripest,
would have plotted against the erasure
—by caprice, of the world, or loss
of his own skill, of his own name
from the list of the world's favorites.
Dick Lancaster did none of these things.
He merely accepted the gifts of the moment, and continued recklessly in alter-
nate disappearances and bursts of
splendid achievement. There was nothing, he argued bitterly, for which he
needed all the fame; so why should he
care to be Fame's courtier? If fame
chose to pursue him, that was another
matter, and beyond his heed.

So, carelessly, recklessly eager for
novelties and excitements, this young
man adventured over the continent of
Europe, gaining everywhere a reputation for devil-may-care-dom and bitterness.

And over many of these things he was
thinking, as he sat in the garden of the
"Kapuzimer." He thought, too, with
something of amused wistfulness of the
Dick Lancaster that had once been himself,—the boy that had suffered twinges
of conscience at the thought of giving up

a Sunday to enjoyment, and had felt forever stained because of things that now
caused him little save ennui. Was it
possible that he had once been like that?
Oh, yes, all things were possible; he
had found that out plainly enough. Indeed, he reflected, if it should happen
to him that the End came tomorrow, he
would have the satisfaction of having
lived his life, completely, fully, even to
satisfy, in half the time that most men
take for that task. Since that night,
after a certain girl had told him to "forget," he had spared himself in nothing
that promised entertainment. With the
old restraints completely cast to the
winds, with nothing but studied reck-
lessness as his Mentor, he had followed
all the promptings of that epicureanism
that he now feigned to consider the only
philosophy.

In all things he was fickle. Just as
the artistic side of him tired quickly of
one place, one set of types, so his animal nature was essentially of the dilettante rather than the enthusiast. Wherev-
er he saw a will-o'-the-wisp he followed;
but it was no sooner caught than he was
repentant of his success. The taste of
pleasure was of the briefest to him; it
turned to bitterness in a moment.

And yet, he mused, with all his varied
experiences, with the feeling of satiety
that sometimes overcame him from sheer
excess of sensations, the fascination of
the town was still upon him. It was
surely in his blood, he speculated. He
remembered with what passionate eagerness, after the final shaking off of all the

old consciences—all those moral skins
that he had shed, and left to rot, over
there, in America—he had come to the
realization of the varied facets of that
bewildering jewel, the town.

He shut his eyes to escape the glare
of the noon-day, and evolve, behind his
closed lids, the aspect of the town after
lamps are lit. The constant current
of humanity, of the swishing of the
women's gowns as t h e y walked,
the rattle of the cabs over t h e
stones,—it all filled him with a passion of pleasure. His young blood went
more quickly at each sight of that surging sea. The crowds going to the theatres and music-halls; the shadows that
flitted hawk-like about the corners; the
colors of the occasional uniforms; he
drank in the picture thirstily. Both the
artist and the man were joined, too, in a
passionate eagerness for beauty; he had
been known, in his folly as men may
call it, to walk a mile so that he might
the more often meet an attractive face
again. The vision of a beautiful female
figure, of a well-fitting gown, gave him
an almost painful joy; he felt that charm
of mere feminity most acutely and cov-
etously.

And yet, with all, he had been a lonely
creature. His pleasures were evanescent
and he was ever constrained to browse
upon fresh pastures. From this novel
experience, that colorful scene, and that
delightful companion he extracted the
essence all too soon; and the dregs
he ever avoided. In his mind there was

a gallery of places, faces and voices—all loves of a moment.

It was a cheerless train of thought that he found himself in. But, as he sipped the pale *Mai-trank*, the glad reflection occurred that the world was very large and that he had seen very little of it so far; there were still plenty of things left that were new to him. Surprise would not die for him just yet.

He was watching the rainbows that glimpsed in and out of the streams of cool water that the fountain, in the square, was sending up into the sunlight. And as he was so engaged, there came to his ear the sound of men's voices, speaking English with an unmistakable American accent.

He turned about.

One of the men was Wooton. As they came nearer, he recognized the other as Laurence Stanley. They were coming directly toward the garden, and in another instant they had seen him. Stanley put on his prince-nez. Then they hurried up to him with a flourish of hands.

"Why, God bless our home," laughed Wooton, "if here isn't our famous young friend, Dick Lancaster, the talk of two continents! I'm glad to see you, mighty glad."

"Stanley," said Dick, after they had all shaken hands, "what are you doing here? Where's Mrs. Stanley."

"My boy, I'm enjoying myself. I presume Mrs. Stanley is doing the same. For reasons not necessary of explanation to the mind capable in deduction we are not, at this moment, breathing the air of the same hemisphere."

"Will you fellows take a bit of lunch? We ought to celebrate this meeting with the famous, etcetera, etcetera," said Wooton.

"Look here," said Lancaster, a trifle coldly, "I'd just as soon you'd drop that adjective business. Here's the bill of the play, Stanley." He handed the *carte-du-jour* over.

While they were discussing their luncheon, chatting of the various causes that had brought them together, and recounting stories, and adventures, Wooton rose solemnly, after a few moments of reflection, and held out his hand to Lancaster. "I want to shake hands with you," he declared, "as with a genuine thoroughbred. I've been listening to you, watching you, and—but that was a long time ago,—hearing about you. You're not the Lancaster I knew."

But, for some strange reason, Lancaster did not hold out his hand. He pretended to be engaged in lifting his glass to his lips. Then he said, "I don't consider that a compliment."

Wooton scowled a little to himself, but passed the matter off lightly enough. "Well," he continued, "at any rate it does me good to see you. How are they all? I've not been back in years, you know." The reason for, and occasion of his exodus did not seem to touch him with the least shade of annoyance.

Lancaster looked at Stanley. "I'm not the man to say. I left there almost a year ago. Stanley was still there then. Stanley, tell us the news from home."

"Yes," was Stanley's reply, "and a nice lot of speculation there was about your sudden disappearance, Dick. There were all sorts of rumors. Some of them hinted at affairs of the heart." He caught the look on Dick's face, and stopped. "However, that's not to the point, I suppose you're thinking? Well, now let me see: they're all about as usual, I think, except, of course, Mrs. Stewart."

The others both started a little.

"Yes. Her husband died in January. She gave up the 'salon' of course; in fact, I think she went abroad."

Lancaster wondered what she would say to him, were they ever to meet. She must have heard about his sudden leap into public notice, his vagabondian ways, his reckless career. He became moody, abstracted. The others were not slow to observe the change in him.

"Stanley," said Wooton, "its time we left the great man to his thoughts. He is evolving a new and fearful sketch. Hope we've not intruded." They got up and were for leaving him, but he protested, and they all strolled away together. He accompanied them to their hotel, and then sauntered off for a stroll in the *Thiergarten*. He found a bench that gave him a view of the sandy ditch wherein the children played all day long in the sun-light, while their nurses sat placidly knitting or reading. It attracted him immediately, this picture of the little bare-legged youngsters in their quaint German attire, digging about in the sand, shouting and laughing and fighting, and all living in the evergreen country of make-believe.

He began to draw some rough sketches. So engrossed was he that the sun had sunk behind the trees before he remembered that he had promised his two townsmen to go to the "Linden" theatre with them. He got up, looked at his watch, and hailed a passing Taxometer.

CHAPTER XV

IN the days that immediately followed, these three were together a great deal. Presently Stanley drawlingly, announced that he would have to be packing up; his bank account was getting low, he declared, and he would be forced once more to bask in the sunshine of his wife's presence.

The other two still stayed on. Berlin was just beginning to be amusing. People were beginning to return from Marienbad, from Schwalbach, from Heringsdorf. All the theatres were once more open. Summer was saying goodbye.

One day Wooton asked: "Of course you've seen Potsdam?"

Lancaster shook his head.

"Well, then it's high time you did. Leaves beginning to fall and all that sort of thing. The last chance. It's really very worth while. Castles till you can't rest. Babelsberg, Sans-souci, and the New Palace. To say nothing of a bit of Potsdam, near the Barberini Palace, that's almost as good as Venice.

They arranged to make the excursion the first sunny day, and had only to wait until the sun rose again. They chose to travel by boat. It was a splendid journey, in the bright sun-light, past the woods and rushes and villas that skirt the little series of inland lakes between Spandau and Potsdam. They left the steamer at the landing-stage for Babelsberg and went leisurely through the grounds and the simple, comfortable, old place. By the time a boatman had rowed them over to Potsdam, it was luncheon time.

They left the boat riding in the Venice-like waterway, and stepped directly into the garden of the vine-covered, shady cafe that skirted the water for quite a distance. Waiters were moving about and at tables sat family parties, eating and drinking cheerily and honestly. It was one of the things that enchanted Lancaster, this part of continental life, this open-air freedom of taking one's glass of beer, this cheerful way of supping out-doors *en familla*, of devoting to restaurant-garden uses the most expensive corner-lots, of making the passing show of strollers one of the sights that you paid for with your glass.

They chose a table that directly overlooked the water-front. Behind them lay the yellow shabbiness of the Barberini palace, that relic of a king's devo-

tion to a dancer. Below them gleamed
the water. It was by no means an un-
picturesque spot.

"By the way," said Wooton, casu-
ally, as they were discussing the entree,
"I met a friend of your's last summer, a
Miss Ware."

"Oh." There was not much interest
in Lancaster's tone, but Wooton helped
himself to the Rauenthaler and went
on:

"Yes. Rather a pleasant girl. Charmingly unsophisticated. Known h e r
long?"

"We were children together."

"Ah, then she's a country girl, so to
say, eh? I thought so."

Lancaster was deep in thought. The
other continued to ply himself with
wine.

"We had some charming days together," he went on, reminiscently.
"She amused me immensely. The Tremonts were staying at the same place
then, and I used to amuse myself con-
trasting that Tremont girl with Miss
Ware. The one was like an armor-
plate, the other impressionable as wax."

He began to smile to himself mysteriously. "Do have some of this Rauenthaler Berg," he urged, effusively. "It's
really capital!" He ordered another
bottle, and helped himself liberally.
Lancaster was scarcely heeding his companion. He was looking out over the
water. For once, he was forgetting to
be amused.

"As between two men of the world,
you know," Wooton was saying, lean-

ing impressively on his elbow, "it may as well be understood that that Tremont girl is the newest kind a new woman." "Know what she said to me one day? 'The only thing I don't like about love is its consequences!' Nice girls, these new women, eh?" He laughed softly and drank again. Lancaster turned to watch him. The man was showing all the cad in him; the wine was bringing it out. "Women, nowadays," Wooton went on, "make a fad of everything except the homely virtues. They deliver lectures on art, and literature, and posters, and music, and the redemption of the fallen; but they never care for the staple virtues that bring happiness to households. I'm not saying that I'm a model, not by a damned sight, but I have my eyes open, and I think the woman of today is trying to usurp, chiefly, man's prerogative of being a *roue* if he chooses. What she needs is to go to a medical school. Then she knows the difference." He crumbled a piece of bread, and flung it out to the swans that floated down before them.

"I don't mind telling you," he continued, confidentially. "that they were both in love with me, Miss Tremont and Miss Ware. In Miss Tremont's case, I naturally, had no scruples at all. The fact is, I think she took the initiative." He stopped, smiling significantly, and sipping at the yellow wine.

Lancaster's eyes were glowing with anger. The man's brutality was so disgusting! Not that there was anything surprising in these wine-woven state-

ments, for a man who could welch his
debts in the way Wooton did, two years
ago, was hardly a man to suffer from
scruples of any sort; but the very fact
of having the names of people well-
known to him brought up in this way was
nauseating to Lancaster.

"Why don't you drink some of this
wine?" Wooton was holding the bottle
across the table. "No? You're miss-
ing something good, you can bet on that!
Wine is the way to forgetfulness, and
most men would sell their souls to be
able to forget. Don't you agree with
me? That's right. He leered fatuously
at his companion. "I've always liked
you, y'know, Lancaster, always liked
you. Friend of mine, yessir, friend of
mine; you bet! Great artist, too, proud
to know you. But, oh Scott! what a
simple sort of idiot you were when you
first came to town! You'll excuse my
candor; friend of your's, I am, yessir,
friend of yours." He proceeded to watch
the swans that glided past them, rip-
pling the smooth water gracefully.
"Beautiful creature," he drawled in
drunken sentimentality, "beautiful creature! Reminds me of that girl's neck,—
that girl I kissed in Schandau. Beautiful
neck, Lancaster, beautiful neck! White,
and smooth, and soft, Moreover, she
had the most adorable lips; extraordi-
narily sweet, I assure you. Lancaster,
I understand you've been rioting all over
this continent, you dog you; but I defy
you to say you kissed any sweeter lips
than those. I defy you to—!" He
sank back into his chair, chuckling to

himself. "Excuse me, didn't mean to be so energetic. Excuse me."

Lancaster half turned his head away from the man and looked out over the water. Where the canal widened out into the lake a crowd of youths were amusing themselves in diving from a considerable height; the sun flashed for one instant on each white body as it gleamed through the air down into the cool canal. From across the water came the voices of sightseers and pleasure-finders. Closer at hand, in the very garden they sat in, the occasional clirring of a sword over the gravel denoted the entrance or exit of an officer; in the warm sun-light all these things combined to make a delightful impressionistic scene. Lancaster turned to it as a relief from his companion.

But Wooton, with the growing persistence of intoxication, was heedless of the other's indifference. He began again, maunderingly:

"I don't deny, y'know, that there's an attraction about the woman of experience. Not for a minute! extremely fascinating person, woman of experience. As good as a comedy to make love to her. But the women of experience grow old, very old; while the fresh young sprigs of girlhood never grow old." He chuckled again. "No; they never grow old. They grow into experienced women. Axiom: I prefer the fresh flower of innocence because it never grows old. Sometimes, sometimes it withers. To wither innocence is one of the most fascinating games in the

world. I wonder how often the aver-
age man of the world has played that
game in his life?" He helped himself
to the wine again, and looked at it lov-
ingly as it gleamed yellow between him
and the sun. "You really should let
me pour you out some of this excellent
vintage," he said, oilily smiling upon
Lancaster, "you really should. There
is a deal of philosophy in it."

Lancaster was now watching the fellow in an increase of amused attention.
With the inflow of the wine the man's
mood changed, from a species of maud-
lin sentimentality to an extravagantly
ornate loquacity.

"Philosophy is one of the fairest jew-
els on the robe of fortune. In misfor-
tune it is marked 'worthless collateral.
When we are well off, we philosophize;
when we are hard up we curse philosophy.
Wine is the only real philosopher. Do
you know, I consider your abstinence.
disgraceful, positively disgraceful. It
argues an unphilosophic mind. . . .
There's that swan again! Beautiful
neck. Such grace! And yet, I prefer
the other one. The other one had a
beautiful face, as well as a glorious
neck. Moreover, the taste of those lips
was positively intoxicating." He looked
solemnly at the glass of wine before
him, and declared, impressively: "As
between the two, do you know, I actu-
ally believe I prefer the lips?" He
gulped at the liquor again. His eyes
strayed dreamily into an abstracted
stare. "Dear Dorothy!" he murmured.

"I beg your pardon?" Lancaster started savagely. He thought he might not have heard aright.

The other blandly continued. "I said 'Dear Dorothy!' That was her name, you know. Her name is almost as sweet as her kisses. Dorothy" he lingered over the syllables—"Dorothy Ware."

"What!" Lancaster half sprung up from his chair. Then he curbed himself, with intense efforts, to calmness. "Did I understand you to say that it was Miss Dorothy Ware?"

"Certainly, my dear boy. Most correct. Oh, yes; remember now: friend of your's. Recommend your taste, my boy, I really do. She—"

"Look here!" Lancaster's voice had grown hard and chill. "Do you mean to say that—all that—is true?"

Wooton noticed the other's repressed agitation, and it quickened this mischief in him. "Most exactly true. Are you —can it be?—are you, h'm, jealous? My dear boy, go in and win; I clear the field. I—only harvest once." He laughed at the thought. And then, in a second, his laughter choked to a rattling gurgle in his throat.

Lancaster had sprung up, white and trembling with rage, and stood over him, squeezing the breath out of the fellow's windpipe. "You drunken, hideous hound you," he crunched from between his teeth, "you rifler of reputations, you damnable dog!" He stopped. His rage scarcely permitted words. "You're drunk, damn you, and you're a puny little brute, so I can't whip you as you

should be whipped. But if you don't
take that back, if you don't say you lied
—I'll—give your burning head the cool-
ing it deserves." He eased his hold on
the other's throat for a time. Wooton
glared at him, breathlessly, with a fan-
tastically ugly sneer attempting lodg-
ment on the lips that still writhed for
air.

"Say you lied!" Lancaster loomed
over him in tremendous wrath.

Wooton glared doggedly. "I shall
do nothing of the sort," he managed to
whisper. His left hand was sliding along
the table to where the glass, half full of
wine, stood. Suddenly he gripped it
and with a wrench, splashed up the con-
tents and the glass, full into Lancaster's
face. The crystal shattered on the
artist's chin, fortunately, and so did but
little harm. Before the crash of the
breaking glass was stilled, and the wine
spent, Lancaster's hands were about the
other's throat again; he gave a swing,
viciously, and flung the body completely
over the low railing.

It splashed into the still waters noisily.
The swans swam away for a moment,
then returned in curiosity. As Wooton
came to the surface, he screamed out an
oath and a cry for help. There was a
boatman at the water-steps of the ad-
joining cafe, and in a few minutes he
had pulled the choking man out of the
water.

Wooton glared up to where Lancaster
stood, still hot with anger. "Damn
him," he thought, "if he were not so
much stronger than I—" But the

thought prevailed, and he told the boat-man to row further down the canal.

To the waiters who had rushed up, Lancaster had been very cool. "*Es handelt sich um eine Wette*," he assured them. The whole thing had been so swift, so silent, that up to the moment of the splash in the water, there had been no eye-witnesses. He smiled at the waiters, paying his bill, and leaving a liberal *trinkgeld*. "*Mein freund hat die wette gewonnen.*" Then he sauntered out with a final fierce glance in the direction of the boat that was turning the corner in the far distance, bearing away the scoundrelisms that lived in Wooton.

When he reached the marble circle of the fountain in the gardens of Sans-souci, Lancaster stopped, and addressed the spray, bitterly: "So that was why I was refused? Well, well! It seems, as I said a little while ago, that there are still new emotions in store for me." He watched the spray turn to mist that was almost invisible. "That is the way with ideals," he mused. Then he turned with a laugh in the direction of the ter-races. "How absurd he looked, in the water!" He went on, laughing quietly.

❦

CHAPTER XVI

THE late John Stewart had, in his lifetime, achieved the dis-tinction of being a model hus-band. He was devoted to his wife in more senses of the word than one; he

was content to appear stupid so she
might shine the more; content to slave
at Mammon's shrine for his wife's sake.
His fund of patience, of tolerance, of
faith, had been infinite. It was in return
for these things that his wife, as he lay
in the dying moments of typhoid, whispered to him, with a tremendous suspicion that she had seemed blind to much
of her fortune, "John, dear John, you
musn't go, not yet. I—I—"

And though John assured her that he
was going to get well, the next day
found the promise broken.

Mrs. Stewart, after his death, realized all that he had been to her, all that
she, except in his loving fancy, had not
been to him. And brooding over such
recollections she began to feel the ban of
morbidness, the old rooms, the dear, familiar haunts that had once known his
voice, were peopled now with sadness,
and she resolved to seek escape, for a
time at least, from these living voices of a
silenced lip. She had some cousins in
London; she determined to travel, to visit
them. With her went her nearer cousin,
Miss Leigh, whose whimsical, cynical
sincerities she loved the while she com-
bated them.

So, in the spring, they found themselves in London, then harboring the
whirl of society at its swiftest. But that
had palled on Mrs. Stewart, and she
dragged Miss Leigh off for an apparently aimless tour through Wales, and
the Lake district, and on up to Scotland.

September found them in St. Andrews.

Although it was one of the months that constitute the "short season" of that dear old academic village, it was easily possible to escape the crowds of golf-enthusiasts that studded the links with their glaringly colorful costumes. The old castle, the ruins of the cathedral, the legends of the historic, bloody occurrences that had taken place here for religion's sake,—all these were full of charms to these two American women, saturated, as is nearly all that Nation, with a peculiar, wistful reverence for things antique.

There were drives, too, that gave opportunities for enjoyment of the Scotch autumn scenery. Along the banks of the Tay, with the solemn Crampians showing dim in the distance.

Mrs. Stewart loved to sit in the silent coolness of the college quadrangles and dream. It seemed to her that only for such places were dreams fit companions.

One day, they were sitting together on the turf that once had marked a cathedral wall. Miss Leigh was reading; Mrs. Stewart idly watching the breakers roll up to the cliffs.

"I beg your pardon!"

The two ladies looked up, and turned to find Lancaster standing before them, with his hat off and a look of amused surprise on his face.

"Well," said Mrs. Stewart, shaking hands heartily, "the world is small as ever, is it not? It's like home, seeing you!"

"It strikes me the same way." He sat down beside them. They noticed that he was browned and furrowed; the marks of travel, the brace of different climes, the scars caught in the thick of life's battle were all sharply dominant in his externals.

"We ought to feel honored," smiled Miss Leigh. "You are such a celebrity nowadays! We have heard the most weird anecdotes about you of late, you know. You are pictured as the Sphinx and the Chimera in one."

"You are still," he answered, "as cruel as ever."

"But we really feel very proud of you," said Mrs. Stewart. "We know each other too well, I hope, to veil our honest opinions. I admire your work immensely; but I think you're terribly bitter sometimes.

"Ah," he laughed gently, "I'm glad it strikes you that way. Bitterness is the only taste that lives after a complete course of life. But we really must talk of something less embarassing than myself. Do tell me the news! How are all the dear familiars?" He paused, and lowered his voice a little. "If it pains you," he said gently, "let us talk of other things. I—have heard. Believe me, I am sorry, very sorry. It is a poor word, but—" he stopped as she looked up at him gratefully for an instant, and then said with an effort at cheerfulness:

"Oh, they were all well, when we left."

"Yes," put in Miss Leigh, "and doing about the same old things. Mr. Wreath still expounds, in and out of season, the doctrine of his own surpassingly correct theories on veritism in literature; and incidentally takes all occasions to assail the sincerity of every other living writer. He's an amusing man, and if he had only been given a sense of honor he would find himself an ever re-direct jest. Clarence Miller has written another novel, and all society is wondering whether it will be translated into Magyar or Mongolian. He calls it "Five Loaves and Two Fishes." His brother-in-law has composed another comic opera that some people have the originality to declare original. And—but why continue the catalogue? It's just the same ridiculous circus it ever was."

Lancaster laughed. "Thank you. That's really a volume in a nutshell. I wonder if the performers in that circus really know how amusing they are?"

"Oh, yes," said Mrs. Stewart, "but they keep it up nevertheless. Of course, it's only when one gets away from it that one really gets the most entertaining focus on that sort of a thing. I'm sure," she sighed, "I don't seem to belong to those ranks at all, now." She shivered a little. The sun was setting, and a chill breeze blowing off the sea. "I'm a fraid we must go," she said, rising, "but you must be sure and come to see us." She gave Lancaster a small card, and then, with smiles and bows, and rustling of skirts, they were gone.

In the weeks that followed Lancaster availed himself of the privilege accorded in Mrs. Stewart's invitation as often as possible. The three were together almost daily, if only for a few moments. Lancaster was busily employed, the while, in fixing in black-and-white some of the types and features that prevailed in this fashionable corner of Fife. The London and Paris journals soon gave evidences of his industry. Fortunately, but few of these papers found their way to St. Andrews, and Lancaster's love of incognito was not disturbed. Sometimes the artist would disappear for days; a fishing-boat would be his hope for the time, and he would drink in the free winds of the sea, and the passing joy of that toilsome life of the fishermen. The winds and the freshness of the life were like a tonic to him, but he knew that it would presently pall and he would give way to the fever for the metropolitan whirlpool.

Occasionally Miss Leigh preferred to remain in her apartments, leaving Mrs. Stewart to stroll along the links alone with the young artist. "Do you know," remarked Mrs. Stewart, on one such occasion, "that my cousin's tremendously fond of you?"

Lancaster looked up in surprise. Then he gave a short laugh. "She's tremendously mistaken," he said, "I'm not the sort that anyone should be fond of—now." He looked out over the sea. "There goes a steamer. I suppose it's the Aberdeen boat." He watched it wistfully.

"She thinks," continued Mrs. Stewart, heedless of his abstraction, "that you are a young man much to be envied. Already you have a name that is known far and wide, and all life is yet before you. She —"

He interrupted, bitterly: "Life is all behind me," you should say. All, all! I have tried everything, the good and the evil. The one broke my belief in all things; the other gives me the belief that the only thing to do is to laugh. Strange! I heard that phrase first in your drawing-room, Mrs. Stewart! Suppose we sit down. These rocks are fashioned delightfully for easy chairs."

The sun was burnishing the water with a lustre of copper. The sea-gulls moaned as they circled about hungrily. The breakers hissed sullenly below them.

"My philosophy," he went on, after he had seen that Mrs. Stewart was comfortably seated, "is very simple, now. Laugh! That is the text of it."

She mused in silence. "You used to be so different," she murmured, presently. "You were, not so long ago, at the other extreme. You thought everything was solemn, awful, important; that there were majestic duties in life, splendid obligations, and splendid things to live for. Now, — you say it is all a jest, and the only thing to do is to laugh. I think you have had too much curiosity."

"Perhaps. Curiosity is a guide that takes us into a labyrinth and leaves us there. But why," he shrugged his shoulders impatiently, "why must we be forever talking of this hapless personage, me? Suppose we talk, instead, of you?"

"Oh, no. You are the interesting one. You are a study. I should like to help you. I think you are doing yourself an injustice : letting yourself drift as you are. Your fame, alone, won't bring you happiness."

"I'm not expecting happiness."

Mrs. Stewart watched his face, hard set, with it's bitter drop to the right corner of the mouth, and something of pity came to her. "Once," she went on, "it seemed to me that there was a woman who meant for you the same thing as happiness."

"Perhaps." His voice was as hard as before. "That was a very long time ago, — counting by experiences. Why talk of marriage? I don't think I could stand it for an instant; I don't think any woman could stand me. As I once was — that was different."

"Some women are very patient."

"Yes. And then I should go mad until they came out of their deadly patience into something more exciting. A woman's fury would amuse me vastly, I think." He twisted his stick into the rocks, and outlined vague designs in the sandstone. "Why, supposing, for the sake of the argument, that I asked you to marry me, you would, I am sure, consider me a madman to expect you to make such a fool of yourself?"

She flushed slightly. "Merely for

the sake of the argument, I don't say that I would do anything of the sort. I might consider it ill-timed, inconsiderate."

"Ah, I beg your pardon, humbly. I realize that deeply. Merely, I said, for the sake of the argument. I want to show you the utter hopelessness of my position. Suppose then, that I asked you that question, what would you tell yourself? That I was a man, young in years, old in experiences, soured in thought and taste, bitter in mind, selfish, a slave to the most egoistic of epicureanisms. A man who considers nothing too sacred for laughter, or too ridiculous for tears. A man who is a perpetual evidence of the corroding influences of flippancy; whose very art, even, is merely a means for amusement. No, — you, clever, shrewd, adaptable woman of the world though you are, would realize at once that to enter into a life-partnership with a man of that sort were to invite immediate misery. Think: the man would be ungovernable, save by his moods; when he should be at home acting as host to a dinner-party he would be tramping the moors in a wild passion for solitude? A man who would perpetually fling at his wife the most mordant of sarcasms, merely for the pleasure they caused his powers of creation. If a biting jest came to him, he would hurl it at his wife, without malice, but because she happened to be present. Not even the cleverest woman in the world can decide between the words and the motive in a case like that. No; this man has

fed too much on the lees of disenchant-
ment to be himself aught but a sorry
devil of a jester."

She sighed. "You have the modern
disease in terrible development—self-
analysis. It seems to me to be quite as
cruel as vivisection. And I think you
exaggerate your vices. After all—I may
speak frankly, may I not? I am a woman that has ever kept her eyes open—
you represent nothing so very dreadful.
You are young, impetuous; you have had
the bandages of stern puritanism rough-
ly torn from you, and you have had a
little of what the world calls 'your fling!'
You realize yourself far too much. You
are not one whit worse than others. All
men worship, for a time, at the shrine of
their animal natures, I suppose. But instead of letting the thought of it all
drive you further and further into bitterness, why not resolve to shake off the
whole cloak, and put it back into the
limbo of thinks henceforth to be avoided?" She paused, and looked at him
with a smile. "Get married. I believe, in spite of your fears, that you
will make a good husband. Believe me,
you will be a much better one than if
you had never taught yourself the re-
volting nausea that the other side of
life brings."

"Marry?" he repeated, why do you
harp on that? I tell you, there is no
one, no one at all! Unless—" he looked
over the breakers to the setting sun,
" unless there were a woman somewhere that could understand and forgive. A woman that knew something

of the world, of the stings of experience and the hollowness of hope. With a woman like that I might become the owner of the new youth, might sink all these bitternesses, live earnest in ambition and . . ." But there is no such woman, none. . . . . A sudden light flashed into his eyes, and with passion he continued, "Except--yourself. Yes-- you are the only one. You know; you understand. Oh, listen to me, listen! Why tell me that this is a sacrilege, an insult to a memory. Do you suppose I don't know that? I do; I feel it deeply; but I also feel that I am pleading for a helping hand, that I see in you the only chance of safety, that you mean for me a new life, and that I must tell you so now, before the opportunity is gone. Oh, don't tell me I'm a coward—I know that, too, well enough. I confess it; I am a coward, a broken-hearted cur." He groaned, and getting up, began to walk slowly up and down before her. "Is it so impossible? I would—you yourself admitted that hope!—improve. Is there no hope?"

"What a boy you are, what a boy! You have all the headstrong, passionate eagerness of youth, and yet you pretend to play the wearied liver of many lives! No, Dick," her voice grew gentler, and it came to him like a pleasant harmony, "we will do nothing so foolish. You and I are always to be very good friends, and we will help each other always, but not that, not that! You are too young; regret would come to you all too soon. No matter how nicely each of us were

to fashion his or her temper to the
other's, there would come that thought:
for the hope of mere comfort I have
sacrificed an idol. For, Dick, think,
think! Dorothy Ware! Do you think
l have not watched you, found you out
long ago? What was it, Dick, a tiff?
A refusal?"

He stopped in his sentry-go, and began to whistle, softly, '*La donna e Mobile.*'
"I—I beg your pardon," he added, hastily, "I fear I forget my manners."
Was it a refusal? you ask. Well,—perhaps, perhaps not. At the time, I
thought it was. Since then I have found
out things—things--Bah, what does it
matter!"

"Go on," she said, "tell me!"

"In Germany, I met Wooton—"

She interrupted. "Ah, yes; I remember a terrible cruel picture you drew of
a man at a cafe table, drinking. It was
his face, unmistakably. Why did you
do that?"

"That was—only an afterthought.
Well, he had been—drinking, and he
talked a good deal. Some of it was about
—Miss Ware."

For a moment there was silence.

Then "And you believed it?" she
asked.

"At the time, no. Lord knows I did
not want to. But, afterward, I remembered the look on her face when she
gave me that last refusal. It was a
strange look; it meant more than I could
account for, at that time. Yes," he
sighed, "I believe it. Why shouldn't
I? I know how vile a man may be; be

a woman only half as weak, or half as
'new,' and she is a thing for loathing."

"Hush! What a conventional man it
is, after all. Always the same old tune,
one thing for the man, another for the
woman! Listen: I know Dorothy Ware,
better, perhaps, than you do; I know
her later self, you only know her as a
child. There are great points of similarity between you two. She has much
of your absurd sensitiveness; self-tor-
ment is one of her vices. She is very
much given to making mountains out of
molehills. She—"

"No, no," he interrupted, wearily,
"I tell you I believe it. All, all of
it!"

"Well," she said, somewhat angrily,
"and suppose you do! What then! Who
are you, that you should judge?"

He winced slightly, but then shrugged
his shoulders. "Oh, of course, of
course; I've heard all about that. But
it won't do, in practice."

"Won't it? Let us put the cases
plainly, for comparison's sake: You are
a young man that has had more than his
share of selfish indulgence; you have
thrown aside all scruples and done everything and anything you pleased.
Your actual transgressions of the com-
mandments we will waive; there is a
greater crime: you have allowed yourself to become a soured, bitter, heart-
less creature, fit only to disseminate
scorn and distaste. She, the woman in
the case, once, we will say, allowed her
senses to oust her sense. Ever since,
she has suffered agonies of regret. Un-

like the man she has not told herself
that she might as well let fate have it's
play out. She is as sweet as the dew of
Maytime, and the slight trace of sadness only needs the touch of love to fall
and almost fade. I think she loves you;
I am not sure—she is a woman, and it
is hard to say. As for you, in spite of
everything, you love her. You coward!
Why don't you ask her again? She will
tell you that it is impossible, of course.
She will say there was once another.
Then, unless you are a greater coward
than I think you, you will tell her
that compared to yourself she is as pure
as the driven snow, and you want nothing, only her forgiveness for yourself."

He was still stubborn. "It is the old
story," he said, "one has heard it all
before. The woman is to be put on a
par with the man; there is no actual difference in ethics. But I once saw it
tried; I shudder when I think of it. To
be sure—the woman was notorious."

"Ah! How can you compare the
cases? And yet—" she laughed a trifle
bitterly,--"in this case the man is notorious." She watched him wince under
the callousness of triumph.

"Think," she continued, "what she
could be to you, how she could help
you; how you could help each other!
The happy days and dreams together,
the planning for new artistic achievements, the sweet companionship of a
soul capable of understanding! Instead
of—what? Fierce flights into forgetfulness; pursuits of vanishing pleasures,
palling desires; short triumphs in art

merged into long revulsions from life!
It seems, to me, a fair exchange!" She
rose, as if to end the subject. He put
her shawl about her shoulders, and they
walked slowly back to the village, talking of other things, gaily, lightly, insin-
cerely.

CHAPTER XVII

LANCASTER said goodbye on the
following morning, and by noon
he was in Edinboro'. At the
Travelers' club he found a letter from
the firm of publishers, at home, that had
lately been using a great many of his
sketches. They took the liberty of in-
forming him that owing to the pop-
ularity of his work they had thought
proper to open an exhibition of his
original sketches in the Museum Art
Galleries. While they were aware that
possession of these originals was entirely vested in themselves, they had decided
to lay aside a share of the receipts from
the exhibition and sale for him, as a
courtesy royalty. Lancaster folded the
letter up, drummed on the table for a
second or two, and then went out to get
a paper. It had occurred to him that,
if he sailed for home at once, he could
reach there before the exhibition closed.
It would be a grim bit of humor to appear there in person, and listen to the
comments of the very people who, a
year ago, would have considered him
and his work beneath their notice. Now,
with a European reputation, his stock,

so to put it, had gone far beyond par in his native country. Besides,—the memory of the things that Mrs. Stewart had said to him refused to pass from him— there was Dorothy! He would see her again; he would put his fate to the touch once more.

It had been a white night that had passed between his conversation with Mrs. Stewart and his departure from St. Andrews. He had lain awake listening to the hissing of the sea over the rocks, and recounting the arguments that affected his feelings toward Miss Ware. Now, it had seemed to him that she represented for him the one chance of happiness; that the touch of sadness that had come to her would make her but the more merciful to his own past. Then, again, the old bitterness, the old distaste came; he could not escape the thought that the old conventions teach, that one step aside means, for the woman, eternal disgrace. Well, and even if the old conventions said so a thousand times, were they to bind him now, when they had so long been thrust away by him in scorn? At any rate, the torment of these conflicting thoughts was to be avoided. He must decide upon one attempt or another—the return home and the repetition of a certain question, or the effort to continue more steadfast than ever in the philosophy of laughter.

He decided for the return to America.

No boat left Liverpool for two days. In the interval he roamed about the most beautiful city in Scotland, enjoying the memories and pictures of the past that Holyrood, the old Castle, and John Knox's house brought up. The autumn sun turned Prince's Street Gardens, and the Scott Monument into a green and gold and flowered picture that he remembered no equal to, in his wanderings through the capitals of Europe, Prince's Street, he maintained, was the prettiest thoroughfare in the world. He left it with regret.

His voyage across the Atlantic merely gave him material for a study of the gowns adopted by the fair ocean travelers, and several chances for cynical representations of the humors of upper-deck flirtations. Otherwise his journey was as monotonous as the luxuriance of the modern travel could make it.

It was morning, when after another fatiguing journey by rail, he reached the metropolis that held so many mixed memories for him. He went straight to the Philistine club, and took some rooms there. The servants hardly knew him. He had, it was true, changed a great deal. He was browner, thinner; there were deep lines about his eyes and mouth.

The first man he met in the smoking-room, after he had refreshed himself with a bath and a lunch, was Vanstruther.

"Why," said that gentleman, after a long, puzzled look, "dashed if it isn't Dick Lancaster!" "Come into the light, most noble genius, and let me gaze upon you. You—you put bright crimson tints on all the effete European cities, didn't you? I declare it's good to see you again! You've seemed a good deal like a myth lately, you know; no one ever seemed to know just where you were, or whether you were alive at all."

They walked up and down the room, asking and answering such pleasant questions as come between two familiars after a long absence.

"Oh, there's not much change," Vanstruther was explaining, "except in yourself. You'll be no end of a lion, I'm afraid. Have to do a couple of paragraphs about you myself, just to scoop the other fellows. Give me a text or two. Oh, but you have hit the fad in the exact centre, somehow! I'm not saying a thing against the real value of your stuff, but the fact remains that this whole blessed nation is fad-mad just now, and it simply has got to have a fad or quit. Your European reputation came along just about the time the fad for the newest English novel was dying. You went, so to say, with a whoop. One can't pick up a Sunday paper now but what one finds weird, impossible interviews with you; descriptions of your favorite models, or reproductions of your newest sketch. You are depicted as the founder of a new style; they talk of women as being "Lancaster-like," and you are a pest generally. In print, I mean, of course, only in print. You are about to furnish my own dear self with material for about a column, so I shouldn't call you a pest; but from the standpoint of the reader, rather than the penny-a-liner, I abhor you!" He made a gesture of aversion, laughingly.

"You want to know about the old guard, do you? Well, Stanley is still the same dismal distiller of cynicisms that he ever was; his trip abroad only seems to have made him worse. Belden? Oh, he plods along in the same old way, drawing bloody battles for the dailies, and making all creation look like the prize-ring 'toughs.' We have the same old Sunday evenings up at his house, too; his wife's turned out well, as far as one can see. He certainly doesn't look unhappy. We were all up there not long ago, Marsboro, Stanley and myself. Mind you, I never take Mrs. Van. I'm about the same as ever, too. I've got a blood-curdling dime-novel on the stocks just now, and the 'season' is beginning for the winter, so I'm not likely to have much time for idle trifling for a while. Oh,—did you see Mrs. Stewart while you were abroad? Thanks! That'll be another scoop on the rest of the society editors. Hallo! three o'clock,—got to be off to the office—see you again!" He rushed off, leaving Lancaster smiling at his frank, jerky sentences.

Lancaster sat down and took up the morning paper. Before long the advertisement of his exhibition at the museum met his eyes. It occurred to him that if what Vanstruther had said was only in part true, it would be wise for him to go and take a peep at the show this very afternoon, before people knew he was in town.

The place was crowded with well-dressed men and women. They flowed in and out in a constant stream. They held catalogues in their hands, and chatted volubly. In front of one picture, whereon was depicted a London music-hall scene, there was an especially large gathering. .

"He's so dreadfully cynical, don't you think so?" one man was saying to the girl that was with him. "I really think he ought to be called a caricaturist."

"Oh, but, after all, it's nearly all true, you know. Look at the expression on that gallery-god's face, will you!"

"Wonder what sort of a chap he is personally?"

"Oh—impossible, I suppose. Although I ought not to say that; nothing is impossible nowadays, there never was such a run on intellect. I never saw anything like it! It positively seems as if society was intellect-mad. Singers, actors, painters, writers—all sorts of queer people go everywhere now, and that isn't the worst of it! The society people won't be content with just playing at 'society' as they used to: they want to sing, and paint, and write, too! It's awful! I'll have to go on the stage, or something of that sort, myself, if I want to keep up with the procession."

Lancaster moved away from that corner. It was amusing, certainly; but it was also painful. What pleased him more than the overheard conversations were the little labels, displaying the word "SOLD" that decorated many of his sketches. It was balm to him to think that these moneybags, these puppets mumbling set phrases, were being despoiled of some of their wealth for his sake.

Walking over to the wall whereon hung the sketch for which Wooton had been the unconscious model, Lancaster heard a voice that seemed familiar.

"It certainly looks like him," the voice was saying. "That would be a wanton brutality."

It was Miss Tremont. Lancaster flushed angrily. What had she to judge by? It was Mrs. Tremont who was accompanying her daughter; the elder lady moved away, that moment, to speak to an acquaintance. Miss Tremont remained in front of the picture of the drunkard, her brows moving nervously.

Lancaster stepped close up to her.

"If I were you," he said quietly, but distinctly, "I should go and look after him. He needs it."

The girl started quickly, turned momentarily pale, and then, seeing who it was, nerved herself to stony calmness. "How dare you?" she said twisting her catalogue into shapelessness.

"Oh," he laughed, "I really mean it for the best. As you see—" he looked sneeringly at the sketch—"he's not the pink of sobriety. And when he drinks, he talks a good deal. He sometimes talks about—you, for instance." He paused and seemed engrossed in nothing save the smoothing out of the wrinkles in his gloves.

"You coward!" If intention could

have killed, Miss Tremont's eyes committed murder.

"True; I fear for you both. And I take such an interest in you! But I believe he will make an excellent husband —for you!" He lifted his hat, with a fleeting mockery of a smile, and left her before the picture, staring, trembling.

"That," he told himself, "was wanton brutality number two. But she should not have judged me!"

He left the galleries, taking with him a feeling of scorn for himself, that he should have put himself on the level of the praise or blame of the fadists in such a public way. Yet, he reflected, it had been not of his own seeking.

The afternoon was already touched with the darkening shadow of evening. The town roared and hissed and seethed in all it's wonted fervor; the chill-hardness of its material manners were painfully evident to Lancaster as he came from the comparative quiet of the picture-galleries. He contrasted the grim roar of the place with the smiling, careless, jovial glitter of those other towns he had lately enjoyed; for the bright cheer of the boulevards and the gardens and the open-air cafes he found the sky-piercing buildings that shut out the sunlight, hemmed in masses of money-mad humanity, and extended apparently to all the horizons. For the strolling gayety he had grown to love so; for the ever-changing current of picturesque triflers, idlers and dandies,—he had received in exchange a breathless surge of anxious, nervous, straining men and women, plunging wildly down the slopes to an imaginary sea of gold. Something of the old repulsion made itself felt in him; he foresaw that it would never again be possible for him to endure life here. That other glittering, careless, joyous maelstrom,—perhaps; this one, never! He realized that while for future generations it was possible, for himself the hope of finding an American metropolis tinged with aught but the feverish strivings after riches was utterly vain. He tried to argue with himself about it; to persuade himself that it was a nobler sign, this one of the masses all honest in labor and in pursuit of it's fruits, than the evidences of inherited wealth, or quiet content with small means, that were the prevailing notes of older countries. But he failed. His temperament rebelled; he loved the smooth, the finished sides of life; the artist in him rebelled agianst the commercialism of his native haunts. If it should be the decree of fate that he continue to seek out life's most distracting enchantments, he would certainly have to bid his native land farewell again. If there were anything else in store for him; if it happened that he be required by Dame Chance to do something more serious than to laugh, to laugh, and laugh— well, that consideration would bear postponement.

It seemed to him, as he walked through the streets that were now beginning to glitter with the white and yellow lights born of electricity and gas,

that these faces were the same faces always, that there was never any change,
from year to year, in the puppets that
paraded on this urban stage. A thous-
and differing types, to be sure; but
a l w a y s the same in their hard,
tense, sinster look of restraint; all wore
the same tiring eyes, the same rounded
shoulders. The same fierce passion for
excitement swam in the eyes of the women. In his morbidness he fancied that
it was as if all these city-dwellers were
life-prisoners, condemned forever to
walk, and mumble and laugh shrilly.

"The metropolis," he told himself,
"is a maelstrom that never gives up it's
human prisoners: it merely changes
their cells occasionally." At which reflection he presently laughed. The old
text came to him: "The thing to do is
to laugh!"

"Yes," he thought, "but it's harder
here than anywhere else. Much harder."

Arrived at the club, he ordered dinner, and in the short interval, set down
to write a letter to his mother. For the
many months of his absence abroad he
had contented himself with sending her
occasional newspapers, the briefest of
notes, and illustrated magazines. In
none of these missives had there ever
been the real personal, familiar note.
He had given merely the scantest news
of his whereabouts and his well-being.
In the life and the philosophy he had
chosen there was little room for com-
radeships, even with his own mother.
Now, however, with the distance be-

tween them so vastly less, he felt again
some of the old affections that he had
thought to have slain with laughter. In
any,event, he wrote, whether he decided
to remain on this or that continent, he
would pay Lincolnville a visit presently. They would have that dear, delightful talk that the months had despoiled
them of.

As he stepped into the dining-room,
Vanstruther hailed him. "Saw a friend
of yours just now, Dick," he said, "Miss
Ware!"

"Ah," was the reply, given in apparent abstraction, "they still live here
then?"

"Yes. Dick did it ever occur to
you that she's a devilish pretty girl?"

"Oh, look here, Van," said Dick,
laughingly, "I came to feed on solids,
not the lilies of your imagination. The
prettiest thing in the world to me, at
this date, is a good dinner."

CHAPTER XVIII

IT is impossible, even for the most
harassed of human beings, to be
entirely pessimistic after a dinner
that had been well prepared, tastefully
served, and finely appreciated. With
the coffee and the liqueur a warm
glow of pleasant sentiment is sure
to invade the dinner; the dismal
reflections that harrowed his soul
an hour ago have fled at the approach

of that self-satisfied feeling that marks the man that has dined.

By this time the Curacao called for discussion, Lancaster had succeeded in putting away all thoughts of the cheerless philosophy of laughter that he had come to consider at once his salvation and his curse, and was quietly, even hopefully, contemplating the chances in his intended interview with Dorothy Ware.

It was all a question, he had now assured himself, of whether she loved him or not. If not, then all other things were of no consequence. If she did, but yet denied the possibilities of their union, he would venture all things to scatter her arguments to the ground. Nothing else need matter, so she loved him. Who was he that he should ask of any woman the question: What art thou?

He had a hansom called and bad the man drive North. The fierceness was changed a little in the face of the town; it was now the fierceness for pleasure, rather than for riches. Everywhere there were couples hurrying to the theatre, the opera, the concert. Carriages drove swiftly through the glaring streets. The restaurants seemed shining with the eagerness of expectancy. Men in evening clothes walked along, smoking, laughing and chatting. The newsboys were gone; in their stead was a miserable, skirmishing band of Italian tots, who used the papers they carried more as an aid to mendicancy than as stock in trade.

It came to Lancaster for an instsnt,
that he might tell the driver to head for
the Auditorium; he might go in and hear
that charming *Santuzza* whose acquaintance he had made and enjoyed abroad.
He might send her his card; there
would be a renewal of pleasant fascinations, forgetfulness of all other things—
and laughter! He lifted up his arm, to
tap for the driver's attention; his cuff
caught in the window-curtain, and the
accident, slight as it was, recalled him
to himself. He shuddered a little; the
things that shaped the courses of men's
lives, he thought, were so absurdly in-
significant!

When the cab stopped in front of the
house that the Wares occupied when
Lancaster was last in town, a flood of
brilliant light flooded out upon it from
the windows and the hall. It was evident that there was an entertainment in
progress. Could it be that they had
moved? Lancaster, paying the cabman,
told him to wait for a moment, for further orders.

But the maid, answering Lancaster's
ring, settled the doubt in his mind.
Miss Ware, she said, was receiving. He
gave his name, dismissed the driver, and
entered, feeling a little annoyed at having fallen upon such an occasion.

But presently Miss Ware appeared,
radiant in a rosehued gown, and wistful
happiness shining in her eyes.

"We thought you were thousands of
miles away," she smiled. "What a
will-o'-the-wisp you are! Mother will
be ever so glad. We are going back to

Lincolnville soon, you must know; and this is our farewell reception. Everyone has been so kind to us; we felt we must do something in return."

"To think," she added, looking up at him shyly, "that the occasion should bring out such a lion!"

"Don't!" he implored. "Do you really think they'll know—anything about me? They do? Then, for goodness sake I'm someone else—anyone! For I do detest—"

She interrupted him gaily. "Oh, no; you are doomed. I shall introduce you to the most portentous faddists; you shall suffer. That, sir, may be your punishment for surprising me so!" She glided away, and returned with Mrs. Ware.

Never, thought Lancaster, had he seen Dorothy so gay, so cheerful, so roguish. Whence came that playful mood of hers; that mocking, joyous laughter? Talking to this and that person, Lancaster kept his watch upon Miss Ware. He saw her go out of the room, laughing and chattering, and the moment she reached the conservatory, put her hands up to her forehead and press them swiftly over her eyes. The smile went from her lips; her whole form testified to a sudden relaxation of an artificial tension.

A mask, Lancaster told himself, a mask for her feelings. She was agitated, but she determined to hide all that under a cloak of gayety. He understood. Had he not himself tested the expungent qualities of laughter?

As of old, the touch of her hand, the sound of her voice had thrilled him with a sense of wonderful gladness. At sight, at sound of her all the good in him seemed to become vibrant; she was still the star, far above him, that he longed for. The comforts of his cold philosophies, the promises of the epicureanisms he had delved in so deeply —all faded into ashes at approach of this girl.

"We are really very fortunate," a voice behind him aroused him from his reverie, "in having such a distinguished guest with us tonight." It was Stanley, who stood with his hand on Lancaster's shoulder. "Surprised to see me here, are you? Well, to tell the truth, it's only of late that I've gone into these rare regions. I find that it conserves one's pessimism to enjoy the company of one's fellow-creatures. Will you excuse me, I see that man Wreath coming over here. I really can't stand him. He always remarks to me, sorrowfully, 'Ah, Mr. Stanley, I'm very much afraid you're not in earnest!'" Why, the man himself's an eternal warning against being in earnest. There's nothing that spoils the look of a person's mouth so much as earnestness."

In truth, at that moment, just after Stanley had deftly slipped away, Mr. Wreath had solemnly greeted the artist. "You have shown great talent, Mr. Lancaster, great talent. But—" and he beamed reproach upon the other, "why don't you dig deeper?"

Lancaster felt as if he could have

sworn at the man's presuming egoism.
But he merely laughed, and said, "Ah,
you forget what a fellow-artist of mine
once said, *apropos* of cleanliness.
'Wash,' he said, 'no, we don't wash;
we merely scratch and rub, scratch and
rub.' I choose, in like manner, only to
scratch. If I can scratch an effective
creation, why should I dig?"

Wreath shook his head, with a mourn-
ful smile. "Ah, you will agree with me
—later. In the meantime, I want to
talk to you about my next novel. Do
you think we could make it worth your
while to illustrate it for us?" He dragged Lancaster off into the library and
bored him, for at least ten minutes.
From the other room came sounds of
music. Someone was singing. "*In Einem
Kuehlen Grunde*" went the soft, sweet
old ballad. Lancaster promised Wreath
that he would let the writer's publishers know definitely in a day or so,
whether he would undertake the illustrations. He hurried back into the
salon, muttering, as he went.

"Several haystacks; two threshing-
day scenes; several prairie pictures, one
for each season of the year — that's
about what those illustrations will have
to be. Well, I'd do it twice over if that
man would promise to let me alone!"

It was Dorothy Ware that had been
singing. She got up just as he entered
the room. She caught his look, and
smiled to him. "You must take me to
the conservatory," she commanded,
with a pretty air of authority, "for singing is warm work." She took his arm,

and while someone else went to the piano and began to play the ballet from "Sylvia," together they strolled out into the cooler rooms beyond.

"And now," she said, when they were snugly seated upon the cushioned windowseat, "I must tell you how proud mother and I have been of you. Oh, it was so good to read all these praises of you!"

He smiled. " It came," he said, "because I did not care whether it came or not. I was indifferent; and so success came."

"Indifferent? Why, Dick? With such power it is not right to be indifferent. Why—"

"Why should I be anything other than indifferent? For myself? No. I despise myself too much. I consider myself only a means toward amusement. And if not for myself, for whom?"

She was playing with the leaves of a palm that hung down over her shoulder.

" No," he went on, " there was never any motive in it all. It was all sheer play. There was the joy, the delirium of creation; that was a sufficient sensation; beyond that—nothing! It might be different if . . ." He stopped with the word half spoken.

" If what?"

He looked at her swiftly. There was in her face only earnest curiosity and sympathy. " If," he continued, " if there were—someone else. Oh, Dorothy, dear, don't you see? Don't you realize that it is you, you for whom I would work—yes, work and live? Dorothy, tell

me that you are not altogether indifferent. Once—long ago—you said
you might care for me. Then we
were boy and girl; now we are man and
woman. Then again you told me to
forget you. I tried. I tried—all ways
into forgetfulness. I tried to laugh
away you, and all the past; to live only
for the essence of the moment. And now,
Dorothy, why don't you speak?

She gently disengaged her hand from
his. Her face was white, and she could
only shake her head.

"But why?" he moaned, fiercely,
"why? Can you not love me a little?"

She looked at him reproachfully, and
for a moment he thought he divined the
framing of the words, "Ah, but I do
love you," then she merely sighed, and
looked away again.

"Is it," he went on, "that I have put
myself beyond your mercy? Have I become too notorious a vagabond?" He
laughed bitterly. "Well, it is all true;
I am come through all the highways
and byways of life, and I am touched
with the scum of it all. Perhaps you
are right. I am not worthy. And
yet—I only ask for forgiveness, and a
little love. With that, I might—be able
to—sink the bitterness of the days behind. But, as I said, I dare say you
are right. Shall we go into the other
room?"

"Oh, Dick," she sighed, "how hard
you make it! Dick, it is—it is I that
am not worthy." She put her hands to
her face suddenly, and pressed them

feverishly to her cheeks and eyes, and then started as if to go away.

Lancaster took her hand and kissed it. "Dorothy," he said, "Don't talk nonsence! Unworthy of me—of a man who has used the world as a playground, and exhausted his days in satiating curiosity! Ah, no! That is imposible. There is no one, Dorothy — no one, however wretched, who would not be worthy of me."

"You don't understand," she wailed, "you don't understand! I—" she hid her face in her hands again, "I have sinned!"

He put his arm about her, and whispered, "What does it matter Dorothy, if only you love me?" Do you, Dorothy, do you love me?

She sobbed, silently almost. Then she looked up, and, as if she were defining a happiness that could never be, said, "Yes, Dick, I love you." Then, as he covered her brow with kisses, she shuddered in his arms, and again moaned, "But you don't know, you don't understand!"

He smoothed the tears from her eyes, and looked tenderly upon her. "Yes, dear, I do." He burst into a fierce trumpet of rage. "That cad, Wooton, —he told me some damnable lies . . . ! He was drunk . . !"

She shrank away from him. "Ah, then, you see it is quite—impossible!"

"Dorothy," he said, "I am not speaking of that, am I, dear? I am asking you to have pity on me, to help me see that there are bright and tender and true things in life. I tell you that, past or no past, you are as high above me as the stars. Why must we listen to the old shibboleths, Dorothy? Have you not spent a lifetime of regret to atone for a moment of folly? And who am I to judge? I, in whom there is no more of whiteness left, save only that I love you! Consider, dear, if this is not to be, what our lives will be! For me, all the old bitterness, the efforts to drown all things in laughter. For you—memories! But if you say 'yes,' Dorothy, think! How different the world will seem! We will go and live in the country, close to the heart of Nature. All the noise and noisomenesses of this town-world will be shut out; we will forget it. For you, dear, I will work as I never worked before. Think, dear—think of the dear old, silent, restful hills of Lincolnville! How the insects hum in the clear nights; how blue, how deep, how tender the sky seems there; how the very flowers seem to wear more natural faces than do those of town! Do you remember how, in summer, we used to go camping by the river? The simple pleasures, the healthy out-door life—can you not believe that it would make new creatures of us two, Dorothy? The house—think of the house we would plan, the orchard, the garden! And are we to lose all that, dear, for a whim? Dorothy," he held out both his hands to her, "see, Dorothy, I ask you to let me not see happiness only to lose it?"

For another moment she wavered, then with a choking "Ah, Dick, I love you!"

she let him take her to his arms.   He
kissed her shining eyes, and said, fervid-
ly, "Sweetheart, I thank you."

EPILOGUE

IT was in the first beauty of June that
Dick Lancaster brought her that had
been Dorothy Ware home to Lincolnville as his wife.   The village, as I remember, was looking its fairest; the
trees were radiant and profuse of shade;
the grass was long and luscious, the birds
were cheerful and bold.   We welcomed
the two with all the heartiness we had
command of; we had known them as
children, and we had loved their memory always, all through the years they
had been gone. Of Dick's fame we were
immeasurably proud.   We wondered a
little, indeed, that a man so dear to the
world's heart should find satisfaction in
living so far from the pulse of it all.
But, we argued, if indeed, he preferred
Lincolnville, all the greater was the
honor.

Both, as we soon saw, had aged.
Mr. Fairly, who had gone up to town
to marry them, had told us as much,
but we were but little prepared for
the actual evidence.   Those of us,
too, who were permitted closer glimpses
into the life of these two, observed in
the two a passionate fondness for the
fields, for the silence and stillness of
our life there that was something very
different from the matter-of-course ac-

ceptance of those attributes to our existence that existed in the rest of us. It
was as if the place were, for them, a
very harbor of refuge, a hospital in
which to forget old ailment, or regain
old healthfulness. These things, and
many other signs of something wistful
in the affection they bore the place and
the dislike they long showed for leaving
it, made up for me and many others,
something of a mystery. At that time,
I knew nothing of the things that had
occurred since Dick left Lincolnville.

Afterwards, long afterwards, it happened that I came to know all the things
that have been chronicled here. And,
for my part, I came to love them the
more. As Mr. Fairly, who, I suspect,
also knew something of these things,
once said to me, "If one has not seen
the devil, one does not know enough to
get out of his way." I consider that
Dick Lancaster is much more to be com-
mended for the honest life he lives
among us than old Scrattan, the milk-
man, who has never been out of Lincoln
County in his life. And as for Dorothy,
all Lincolnville thinks she is the sweetest woman breathing—and when a village as given to gossip as is this place,
agrees on any such eulogy as that, there
must be potent reasons.

It is an ancient trick, I know, and an
uncommendable, this of chronicling the
lives of two people only up to the church
door. In the lives of most people, I
hear on all sides of me, the tragedy
only begins after marriage. Well, perhaps so. But I hope, for my part, that

for Dick Lancaster and his wife there is not to be much more of battling against the buffets of the world. For them there had been so much of tragedy—the tragedy that is almost intangible, the tragedy that underlies the surface flippancy of our modern life—before Fate chose to let them come together, that it would seem just that thereafter their life be but a pleasant pastoral. As for that I cannot say. I know that Dick's fame grows with each passing year; and that both he and his wife are beginning to lose the look of weariness that was on them when they came back to us.

I have not given this chronicle as an example or a lesson. I do not mean in telling it to declare my belief in the theory that Christ's words "Go, and sin no more!" can be perpetually applied in the practice of modern life. I have transcribed one episode, one group of characters, one set of lives, and having done so, I refer the responsibility whither it belongs to the Being that mapped, that directed those life-threads. I do not mean to say that in like instances, a similar course would inevitably lead to happiness. I only say that yesterday, as I was walking in my garden, watching the blue-jays quarreling in the firs, I heard Dick and Dorothy talking and laughing on their veranda. There was something so infectious about their gladness that I paused and listened, without thought of curiosity, but rather in something of wistful appreciation of their happiness.

"I had not thought," I heard him

215

say, "that the world would ever seem so fair to me."

There was a pause, and I fancied I heard a kiss, but I will not be sure.

"And all," he went on, "is thanks to you."

Again there was a long silence! And then there came a sudden frightened whisper from her: "Dick—do you think we shall ever see—him—again?"

He laughed bitterly. "No, dear. He is too vain, too selfish, too fond of his own safety. Besides—what matter if we did. He belongs to the things that we have forgotten.

Then they turned, laughing into the house, and their voices gradually died from my hearing.

It seemed to me, as I nipped the dead leaves from my geraniums, that to these young neighbors of mine Happiness was showing a smiling face. And whether they had deserved that or no, I wish it may be so always, to the end. —

FINIS